To. Roberta

From Abel

6/30/94

THE ANGELIC MYSTERIES

THE ANGELIC MYSTERIES

A NOVEL

by

JAMES D. SANDERSON

COLONIA BOOKS
1994

Published in the United States by Colonia Books, Post Office Box 4018, Durango, Colorado 81302.

Manufactured in the United States of America

1 2 3 4 5 6 7 8 9 10

Library of Congress Cataloging in Publication Data
Sanderson, James D. 1952 -
The Angelic Mysteries

1. Angels - Fiction. I. Title
Library of Congress Catalog Card Number: 94-70011

ISBN 1-884787-00-2

This novel is a work of fiction.

WITH LOVE

FOR NANCY

THE ANGELIC MYSTERIES

ABOUT THE PARAGON CYCLE

The best of fiction is not plot and character and theme and setting, but illusion. It is the perfect blend of these various elements, transformed by the author in his or her own unique way, that makes magic. There is much that is magic here and in the future volumes of the Paragon Cycle. Whether whisked through secret doors into the realm of angels or evil satraps or the magic theater, or into Hawaiian pleasure gardens, the reader is constantly confronted with themes that are as old as time, and yet as contemporary as this morning's news. The characters are plunged into labrynthian plots that strangely reflect our contemporary social landscape, and are confounded by such extreme changes that their emotions and motives and pathos are laid bare for all to see.

These Paragon novels are always entertaining and thought-provoking, and are often downright shocking. The curious tales they tell take us away from our everyday existence, and force upon us at every turn the rich and many-varied worlds we suspect thrive just beyond our normal field of vision. This fearless approach to reality is a continuation of the great literary traditions of 'A Thousand and One Nights' and Franz Kafka and Jorge Louis Borges. To label them as simple fantasy is to miss their true significance completely. Ultimately they are concerned with the very human search for understanding in an increasingly complex world.

So much of today's fiction is comfortable and predictable. You will find none of that here. These novels are lucid and direct, yet deep and unsettling. There is much that is charming and even sensual in them, but always the distressing undercurrent of change compels the narrative forward. For Humankind to survive, this author seems to suggest, the individual must be ready to adapt to a thousand new realities. At the same time, however, we must never forget the vast wealth of wisdom handed down from other times.

- The Editors

ONE

Life is too long to be this ridiculous:

We were supposed to build a hospital in what was, until recently, a cow pasture. I knew better than to ask why. If they wanted me to know anything they'd tell me, right?

The boss came up to me with a set of plans. "Someday the city is going to grow out in this direction and then there'll be a hospital here ready to serve its needs."

"You're a man of vision," says I.

"Damned right," he said. "There aren't many of us left, either."

"Where will they want it?" I says.

"Right out here," he said, sweeping his arm to encompass the field where the cow flaps hadn't even dried good yet. He was always sweeping his arms around. That's how it is with a man of vision, I guess.

"Which way will they want the front entrance facing?"

"Face it to the west, away from the city. Someday the city is going to grow all around this area here and people will be coming into the hospital from all directions. The hospital will be dead in the middle."

I could just picture the boss over in Detroit explaining this proposition to a bunch of dopes in business suits. They'd all bought into it too, apparently.

"Face the entrance west, you got that?" he said.

"Yes sir," says I. Things were pretty simple for me.

"You're the man in charge out here," he said. "If anything comes up, you make it right. That's what we're paying you for."

After he had gone, I rolled open the plans. This was going to be some monster of a hospital. It was ten stories tall and two city blocks around. That is to say, it would have been two city blocks if there had been any city blocks around to measure it by. I called one of my foremen over. "This is going to take a lot of excavation."

"Yes sir," he said.

3

A week later we were excavating the hell out of that cow pasture. There were dozers and graders and earth-movers and front loaders and backhoes and dump trucks and men with shovels. I saw the boss drive up in his Caddy with the whip antennas and cellular phone and such and he got out and came over. He was wearing his yellow hard hat so I knew we were in for trouble.

"Oh shit," said one of my foremen.

"Yeah," says I.

"How's it going out here?" the boss called.

"Great," says I.

"I thought you were supposed to be excavating this site."

"We are excavating this site," I explain.

"Where are all the dump trucks and dozers?" he said.

"Over there," says I.

"Right." He squinted over in that direction. I swear he must have been blind. "Well, ah, listen, there's been a change."

"What sort of change?" says I.

"Oh, it's not a big change," he said.

"Are we still building a hospital," says I, "or are we going for a day care now?"

He didn't catch my humor. "We're building a hospital alright," he said. "Just like I told you. Only, now we've bought that little stretch of land across the road there, so we're going to build a cancer center too."

I saw some of the men smile at each other. They were happy. This was job security.

"Where exactly is this piece of land?" says I.

He took me over and showed me and gave me another set of plans. "As soon as you're done with the excavation over there, you can move all the equipment over here," he said.

"Yes sir," says I.

The boss left. I called one of the foremen over.

"What is it?" he said.

"We're going to move the equipment over to this side as soon as we're done over there."

"Yes sir," he said with a smile.

So we finished up on the one side of the road and moved the heavy equipment over. While they were busy on that side, we staked out the building on this, the hospital side. About the time we were getting ready to pour the concrete for the footings, the boss showed up. He was wearing his yellow hard hat.

"Oh shit," someone said.

"Belay that," I says. I was a sergeant in the combat engineers before signing on with this bunch.

"How's things going?" the boss called.

"Perfectly," says I.

"That's good," he said. "That's real good."

I knew better than to ask him anything.

He looked all around the building site and nodded his head. He was playing his part. I was playing mine. "You poured the concrete yet?" he said.

"Tomorrow," says I.

"You might want to hold off on that a day or two."

"Really?" says I.

"We've got some changes to make in the plans."

I looked at him for a long moment. The men expected that of me. Then I rolled out the plans on the hood of my pickup. He penciled in the changes they wanted to see made. We were going to have to undo a lot of what we had done, and then redo it in a different way. They were going to shift the whole footing around several feet.

"Can you handle it?" he asked.

"Yes," says I.

"It won't set you too far behind, will it?"

"About a week," says I.

"Good. Good. I knew we could depend on you."

When he had gone, one of the foremen came up to me. "Is everything alright?" he asked.

"Start pulling up stakes," says I.

We pulled up all the stakes, reset the lines, redug the footings, and called for the concrete a week later.

"You're getting paid for it," I heard one of my foremen tell his men. "You're getting paid damned good for it."

We got the footings poured on the hospital and got the cancer center surveyed and staked and the lines set and the footings dug. The center was going to be four stories tall and one city block around. (That is, again, if there had been any city blocks around to compare it with.)

The men really busted their humps for this outfit. We got the
forms up for the walls of the hospital and got the concrete poured.
It was sweaty weather even for western Michigan. It was already
late August. There were days when the air didn't move at all.

We broke down the forms and moved the whole kit and
caboodle over across the road and got ready to start busting our
butts over there when the boss showed up.

"Oh shit," somebody said.

"Yeah," said somebody else.

He was wearing his yellow hard hat.

"Everything alright?" he called.

"Sure," says I.

"You still got that earth-moving equipment around?"

"Right over there," says I, pointing with my chin. He'd have
run his big Caddy right into it if he hadn't seen it on his way in.

"That's good," he said. "You see, there's been a little change
in the plan."

"Has there?" says I.

"We're going to dig a tunnel across, under the road, so that
the hospital and the cancer center will be connected.

"I see," says I.

"It'll be great, don't you think?" You could tell he was
proud of the idea.

"You're a man of vision," says I.

"And there are damned few of us left."

The boss departed. We had to tear out part of the wall of
the hospital, survey and stake the tunnel and set the lines, and then
dig the hole. We had to set the forms and reinforce the whole
thing and then pour the concrete. The men really busted their
humps on that project. Then we got the footings poured for the
cancer center, laid the slab, poured the walls, and broke down the
forms.

Two weeks went by. We kept plenty busy out at the site.
We started getting our ten stories up. We started getting our four
stories up. Girders. Steel beams. Welding. Rivets. Day after
day. It was good, hard, work.

Another month went by. Then the boss showed up. He
came out of Kalamazoo. Often he went over to Detroit for
meetings. Dopes in business suits. You know what I mean.

"Hello," he called. He was wearing his yellow hard hat.

"Hello," says I.

"How are things?"

"Things are fine."

"Any troubles?"

"None," says I.

"We've made a little deal with a farmer just to the east of the cancer center over there." He pointed.

"A deal?" I knew better than to ask.

"We bought him out. It's a heck of a nice asparagus patch. Some fruit trees too. Nice place."

I didn't want to ask. I didn't want to ask. I just looked at him hard. The men expected that kind of thing from me. The boss kept waiting for me to say something. Finally I says, "Are we going to build something over there?"

"They want a tract of houses over there. We're going to house all the employees of the hospital and the cancer center. It's going to end up being a whole complex."

"Houses," I says. "We're not really set up for houses."

"We're going to abandon the hospital for the time being. There's no rush, right? People won't be moving out this way until there are houses."

"Whatever you say."

"We want you to gear up for houses. We may be able to buy another patch of land further east. Then we'll start moving people out this way." He was growing louder with every word he spoke. "With the people will come the need for the hospital and the cancer center."

"You're a man of vision," says I.

"There aren't many of us," he agreed.

"What about the cancer center?" says I.

"What about it?"

"You said to suspend work on the hospital. You didn't say about the center."

"Oh, yeah. Suspend work on that too. Get started on the houses right away. We want houses. Lots of houses."

"You got it," says I.

Once he had taken off, I turned to my foremen. "Houses."

"Houses?" they said, looking at one another.

"Houses," says I.

"Do you really think they know what they're doing?" one of them asked.

"Of course they know what they're doing," says I.

They were all good company men, just like me. I was always a company man. When I was younger, I used to follow the orders given by my dad. Then I did what the army told me. Now I worked for the company. It was simple as that.

Some people like to do things and get credit for them. Others want to do things outside the system. I know where I fall. Anyway, belay all that talk.

Next morning it was houses. A few weeks later I was up on the roof of one of the houses when I saw the boss without his yellow hard hat. He was way off over on another farmer's plot of land and they were seriously talking about something. Of course I knew very good and well what it probably was. The boss was trying to deal the man out of his land. The man kept shaking his head, however.

Later that same day the boss came out to the site. He was wearing his yellow hard hat. "How are the houses going?" he called heartily.

"They're going good."

"I was over this morning trying to make a deal with a farmer just to the east of here."

"I think I might have seen you over there," says I.

"Son of a bitch wouldn't sell," the boss said.

"That wasn't very sporting of him," says I.

The boss looked at me. "You know, I used to build. I started out as a pup on these sites."

"That so?" says I.

"I was damned good, too. Every time I turned around someone was promoting me."

I grunted, not knowing quite what to say.

"You've been doing pretty well yourself," he said. "You're just like me. You've got vision."

I scuffed the ground a second with the toe of my boot.

"Well, anyway, what we're going to do is build all around that son of a bitching farmer. We'll put the squeeze on him. Taxes will go through the ceiling. He won't be able to farm that land any more. We'll show him you can't stand in the way of progress. You can't operate outside the system, by god!"

I had never seen the boss get so emotional before. I wanted to ask if that meant there would be some changes to the changes. I wanted to ask but I didn't want to ask. Finally, I did ask.

"Yes, there will be some changes. I want you to move all the men over to the sections all around that obstinate bastard and build, build, build. We'll freeze him out. He can't say no to change."

The boss left. We moved our crews over to the new lands all around the farmer. The farmer, angered, fired a rifle shot over the heads of some of the men. Sheriff's deputies came out and hauled him away. His kin had him declared incompetent and they got control of the land and made a deal with my boss and made themselves a fine profit.

"You think that old man was mental?" one of the men asked me.

"Hell yes," says I.

So we got the land. The boss came out to the site. He was pleased as punch. He was wearing his hard hat.

"Oh shit," one of my foremen said.

"Yeah," says I.

"Who was that woman?" the boss called.

"What woman?"

"The one who was just there." He looked all around us in an animated way.

I looked around as well. There was no woman.

"She was just behind you. I saw her over your shoulder."

"I don't see any woman," says I.

"Too bad. She was a real beauty."

I shrugged.

"Anyway, you got any tools around here?"

"We've got tools," says I. Tools and equipment and materials were strewn over an area a mile long; from the original site of the hospital. He could see nonexistent women, but not tools.

"There's been a little change to the plan," he announced. He took a set of plans from under his arm and rolled them out on the hood of my pickup.

"No more houses?" says I.

"No more houses," he said.

I wanted to ask, but this time I didn't have to.

"We're going to build a research center."

"A research center," says I.

"Yes, a research center. Have you forgotten the hospital and cancer center already? It'll be a great research lab that can be used in connection with the hospital. It'll be a great boon to mankind. We may, right here on this site, discover the cure for cancer."

"You're a man of vision," I says.

"There aren't many of us around," he said, absorbed in his blueprints. He reached down and jerked his tool belt around straight. "I hope you don't mind, but on this project, I'm going to get involved myself. I think I told you I used to build."

"You told me," says I.

"I kind of miss it," he said. "I've been away from the real building end of construction so long, I want to get the feel of it again."

"I see," says I.

"We're going to need lots of materials," he said. "This center is going to be built all on one level so that scientists won't have trouble getting to work. They can just drive up on whatever side they work on, and go on into their offices. Scientists aren't the only ones who can devise new ways of doing things."

"No sir," says I.

"Instead of being ten stories tall, it'll be ten stories long. It'll be wide, too. Wide."

"Wide. Yes sir."

"We're going to need Portland ASTM C595-Type IS blast furnace slag cement, reinforcing bars, anchor bolts with pipe sleeves, templets... are you getting all this?"

"Got it," says I. We've been pouring concrete for years without having to list every item.

He went on and on in this excited manner for a good half hour. He just kept naming various materials and tools that he thought we were going to need.

Meanwhile all of the men just stood by, waiting for some orders. It was going to be tough getting used to the boss being on the job site. Him and his yellow hat.

Well, this job started just like all the rest of them. We got the surveying done and set the stakes and ran the lines and dug the footings and poured the slabs and the walls. We hoisted the trusses up and nailed on the sheathing and the roll roofing and shingles.

We started on the inside and then the changes started coming in again.

"We've got to make some changes," the boss said.

I looked at him in his yellow hard hat. He had been working right along with everyone else all month.

"What the..." I heard someone say behind me.

"Belay that," I says.

"We need more rooms on that end," he said, pointing to the east.

"Alright," I says. "How many rooms?"

"Lots of rooms. We need maybe a hundred more rooms on that end."

"Damn it," I heard someone say, "we'll never be done with this project."

The boss turned toward the man. "You want to collect your pay, go right ahead. We'll build this place all the way to Kalamazoo if I say so."

"That's right," says I.

He began to show me what the changes to the plans were going to be.

The men continued to bust their humps well into October. It was getting cool by then. "I've seen snow in November," one of the foremen reminded me. "Lots of snow."

"Michigan," I says, shaking my head. "It's a builder's nightmare. We'll be into winter before we even get this research lab roughed in, the way we're going."

"Are you sure the boss is alright?" he asked.

"What do you mean?" says I.

"He's not going mental or something, is he?"

"Nah," I says.

Every morning I go in and the boss is there working his tail off. He's a man driven, that's for sure. I don't know what made him want to come out to work at the site, but he's putting the rest of the boys to shame. They bust their humps, for sure, but nothing like him. He's a hammer-swinging fool. I've never seen anything like him.

He's extending the footing out about another five hundred feet to the east. "We're going to need more rooms," he says.

"We haven't finished the other rooms yet," I says.

"We can finish them over the winter," he says. "We've got to get them going, though. We've got to get them under construction."

It was getting a little strange, I'll admit. Whole sections of the building were being left unfinished while we kept adding more and more onto the eastern side. By mid-November we had run about three miles in that direction. We just kept adding more and more rooms on. We'd partially finish one section and then we'd be adding some more. We ran the roof line out and then left it hanging.

The boss nailed sheathing on one end and forgot to nail the other end. He just left it dangling. The whole project was left dangling. "It's going to snow soon," he tells me. "We've got to get it closed in before the snows come."

I nod my head. What else was I to do? The skies were looking dark all the time. We were getting a little rain spitting down now and again.

It snowed the day before Thanksgiving. Not much, mind you, but it was snow.

"We're going to have to work tomorrow," the boss said.

"But tomorrow's Thanksgiving," I says.

"I know what day it is," he snapped.

"The boys'll want to be home with their families."

"We don't have time for all that," the boss said. "They'll have to come to work. I'll be here, won't you?" He gave me a hard look.

I had to think about it. Then I says, "I'll be here. But I don't have any family around."

"Good."

"Tomorrow's Thanksgiving," one of the foremen protested, when I gave them the word.

"I know what day it is," I yells. I guess I was being a little defensive about it.

"We're going to catch hell at home," he said as he walked away. "I don't know how we can have happiness without a Thanksgiving day."

I would have stomped off somewhere to find a beer but we were way out in the boondocks, and there weren't any towns within twenty miles. Instead, I sat in my trailer and fumed.

Next morning I get out to the site and the boss isn't there. Most of the men show up. Some of them called in sick. After about ten minutes a big Caddy pulls up only it doesn't belong to the boss. A man in a grey business suit gets out of the Caddy and comes down the hill toward us. He's carrying a yellow hard hat in his hands.

"Oh shit," one of the foremen says.

"Belay that," I says.

"Hello," the man calls.

"Hello," I says.

"Are you the man in charge out here?"

"That's right."

"I'm from Detroit. Your boss has been having... a little trouble..."

I don't say anything.

"He's been... having a little trouble. You all came out here on a Thanksgiving morning?"

"That's right."

"You must be a good leader."

"I try," says I.

"Here," the man says. He hands me the yellow hard hat.

"What's this?"

"You're the boss now."

I look around at all the men. They don't know what to think. "Thanks," I says.

The man starts to walk away.

"Hey boss," says I.

"Yes." The man turns to look at me.

"What am I supposed to do about all this?" I nod with my chin back toward the research center and the houses and the cancer center and the hospital.

"Give your boys the long weekend off," he says. "Next week we're going to start building an automotive factory."

"But," (I shouldn't have asked; I really should not have asked), "what about what we've already done here?" I put the yellow hard hat on my head.

"Tear it down," he says.

TWO

I awoke from this episode as from an unsettling dream. Over the past ten years I had become a stranger to myself, it seems. I had been playing so hard at being someone I was not, I had become him. I found that I was a man of reason wrapped in a construction worker's clothing. Even the way I spoke had become rough and foreign. In that one day I had reached as high in my profession as I would probably ever reach, and yet I was not fulfilled. This was not what I had envisioned for myself as a boy daydreaming in the park.

The fact of the matter is, my life had become a riddle I could not solve. How had this happened? I cannot say. Through the long winter I had plenty of time to think about it, though. Somehow I had fallen into this all-consuming routine of work and I had put everything else out of my mind. Seeing the boss go crazy, though, that had set my brain to going.

It felt a little strange to be wearing that yellow hard hat, as you might imagine. Still, one is always safer to continue in the direction one has been going, I say. That hard hat stood for mediocrity, to be sure, but it also represented security. My boss had tried to break out of his mediocrity and look what it had cost him. He tried to go out beyond where he had been before and he went right on over the edge. What good had that done him?

For him, the world was flat after all!

No, it's better to continue on your course. Then you don't have to worry.

Still, I began to wonder what my life would be like if I were to alter my way of doing things a little. The idea began to gnaw at the inside of my skull. What if, for instance, a person were to change the pace of the life he had been living. Instead of watching television, say, how would one's life be changed if one took scuba lessons, or studied a language, or traveled, or embarked upon a second, more interesting career. Perhaps a whole new path would open up. Wouldn't that possibility take some of the sameness out of our modern existence?

These were the questions that kept after me all winter while we cleared that site for the new factory. They were strange ideas, I agree, and a common man like me shouldn't have been thinking them. Better to keep your eyes down and concentrate on your work, I say.

It seems I've spent my whole life pushing against things I don't really understand, I admit. Modern life is just a maze, don't you agree? There's no sense doing a lot of thinking about it. Every time you think you're on to something, you end up at a blind corner or worse, like my boss, you fall off the edge of the world. Reason will get you nowhere today.

My boss wasn't the first one I'd witnessed voyaging out there where the sea monsters swim around just waiting for you to happen by; not by any means. My whole life has been filled with such craziness. (Dare I admit that even to myself?) What I mean by that is, I have been exposed to the enigma of insanity in all its myriad forms since I can first remember.

The earliest whispers of my childhood were about madness. I don't really remember much about it now. There was talk about something going wrong with someone in our family. Something happened that no one really wanted to talk about. Then that person was sent to the state hospital. She had lost her place in life somehow.

Years later my grandmother went to the same hospital. I could see the face of madness reflected in hers. There was that same watery stare and the trembling lips that mouthed words no human would ever hear. Her countenance became withdrawn like a shriveled apple.

It happened this way:

I was then sixteen years of age. Being a new driver, I wanted to show off the old Chevy I had just bought. I wanted to take my brothers for a ride. "Maybe we could drive over to grandpa and grandma's house," I said to my mother. I was anxious to spread my wings and declare my independence at that age. That is to say, I was at an age when I did not know flying was a thing of the past. I still believed in life as adventure.

"I don't know..." my mother said uncertainly. She shot a quick glance over to my father.

He caught her look and held it for a long moment. "There shouldn't be any problem," he said at last. Apparently they knew something that none of the rest of us knew. Still, I was too young and naive to pick up on a thing like that back then.

The drive into town went without incident. Our grandparents lived down near the end of a blind street and they had allowed the hedges to grow up untrimmed over their front windows. Their front yard was a spooky maze, shadowed and hemmed in on every side. Stepping through the rabbit hole of an entrance in the shrubbery was like stepping through into the strange muted world of another age.

Gramps opened the door cautiously. "Ah," he said in surprise. "Look here, Ma, the boys have come."

"The boys?" Grandma shifted somewhere in the darkened interior of the old house. "What boys?"

"The grandsons. Jimmy and them."

He let us in. There was a certain reluctance in his actions but, again, I did not pick up on that then. We went in and sat on the musty old sofa. At first we could not see grandma. She was sitting in the creaky wooden rocking chair. I remember that chair from many Christmases ago, when my brothers and I would rock in it two and three at a time.

Gramps brought us Cokes. The whole place was obscured by darkness. Sunlight was filtered through a series of overhanging trees and shrubs and veiled curtains until it was nearly nonexistent by the time it fell wearily through the back windows over the kitchen sink. He had had to feel his way around the kitchen to get the drinks. Their house had a peculiar moldy smell, too, and if I were to catch a whiff of that smell again now, I would think only of them.

Grandma seemed agitated. Her head was jerking back and forth nervously. She began to rock her chair forward and back in short sprints of emotion.

"Jim's got himself a new git-flivver," Gramps told her.

She slowed down her rocking to look through the gloom at me. Then, without a word, she resumed.

"It's not new," I corrected, to make polite conversation. "It's just an old Chevy. Dad's going to help me fix it up, though."

"That'll be grand," grandpa said.

"Who's your dad?" grandma demanded, stopping abruptly in her chair.

None of us knew quite what to say at first. Why had she asked such a thing?   At last I said, meekly, "It's Duane.   You know, your son, Duane."

"Duane?" she said.   "Everyone told me he was dead.   Why is everyone always talking about Duane when he's dead?"   This last she screamed at the top of her voice.

My brothers and I were stunned into silence.   We had absolutely no way of grasping what this was about, and knew no way to deal with this sudden outburst.   Was she joking?   Did she seriously believe our dad was dead?   We had no idea.

Gramps went over behind her and began gently rubbing her neck.   He said a few words to her that we could not hear and then to us he said, "Bet hasn't been feeling very well lately."

Grandma began mouthing the words that no one could hear and she fidgeted her hands back and forth.   She twined and untwined her fingers nervously.

I don't know, now, what excuse we used to make our hasty exit, but I do remember how upset my father was when we got home and explained the whole situation to him.   "Goddamn it," he shouted, "I ought to kick her butt.   She couldn't hold it together even long enough for you kids to go and visit her."

"No, Dad," I protested, thinking he did not understand the real problem, "she's sick.   She's really sick."

My father's solution to nearly every problem was to bull into it with his awe-inspiring anger.   With many situations this worked very well indeed.   With others, however, it was not so effective. I always felt I needed to protect my father from some things he would never know how to deal with.   This, I thought, was one of those things.

Not long after that my grandmother was committed to the state hospital right there in Kalamazoo.   We went to visit her on weekends. If anything, while she was there, she grew worse.

Gramps couldn't cope with the loss.   He too became strange and paranoid and watery.   "You see that antenna across the street over there," he told me once, pointing at a neighbor's house.

"That's a short-wave antenna, isn't it?" I said.

"That's what he wants us to think. He's listening in on us right now," he said.   "He always listens in."

"What have we got to hide?" I said, thinking he was joking.

He had never been more serious. That is the way it is with that kind of illness, I have since learned. It is always worse than you think by the time you think anything at all about it.

A week later he drank antifreeze in an attempt to take his own life. He called my father on the phone and told him what he had done. My father went over and took him to the hospital to have his stomach pumped. For some reason a big red sore erupted on the end of his nose. That is how I remember poisoning by antifreeze.

Grandpa used to catch live wasps on the side of the house and bite their heads off. I don't know what that has to do with anything except that maybe he was always just a little strange. As a kid I remember thinking how great it was to be around people like him. In his younger days he had run away from home and jumped a train and had gotten involved with union strikers down in Chicago. He was thrown in jail overnight but managed to escape. He hid out in a field of weeds and the cops walked right by him. They never caught him.

Before long he too was in the state hospital. He escaped from there, though, after only a few weeks of captivity. Wouldn't you know it, there was no penning him in.

There was a particular barn in the vicinity of our house that I thought he might go to. He had once told me it would be a good place to hide out, if a man ever needed one. I went out there at night, hoping to find him. I didn't know whether I'd try to take him back in or give him some money and a map to Florida, where at least he wouldn't freeze to death over the long winter.

The barn was back off the road a hundred yards and an owl was hooting in a nearby oak. My flashlight was faltering, as was my resolve. I held it out in front of me, thinking that something terrible was going to happen.

"Gramps," I called. There was no answer. I looked around. No one was there.

A few days later he threw his feet at the back door of an elderly couple, asking them for food and water. They called the police and he was returned to the hospital.

Grandma, meanwhile, had been in such bad shape for so long that we had all forgotten what she was like when she was well. Every time we went to visit her she was sitting on the edge of her bed and staring straight ahead, neither speaking to us nor acknowledging that we were even alive. Then, almost overnight, she made a miraculous recovery. She began to talk again, and to laugh, and to work as a cook in the hospital cafeteria.

After a few months she was released to a home where she could be monitored frequently but not imprisoned as she had been. As soon as she was able, she walked down to the river and threw herself in and drowned.

Gramps took longer to cure but he eventually recovered fully and is alive today. Not long ago he turned to me and said, "I sure miss Bet."

Perhaps as a defense against all that was happening around me when I was younger, and perhaps because I too was a little strange at that age, I turned to imaginary things. My friends, my brothers and I, acted out daily dramas based on recent television shows or any old thing we could come up with. But often I alone turned away from play to books. I loved books. I read everything but I especially loved Hemingway. More than any other author, he could take me away from my suburban world and transport me into other, romantic and adventurous realms.

I didn't know, then, how little Hemingway could prepare me for the labyrinth that is modern life. There were few writers who knew anything about all that. None of them, it seemed, were willing to dip their pens into the bloody inkpot of cold war reality.

It was my great desire to someday become a writer myself. This I knew from an early age. Compared to the heroic Hemingway, however, I knew myself to be a fearful little creep. More and more I withdrew from my family and hid out in my bedroom where I could read of travels and adventures that were beyond my wildest dreams. There, too, I began to compose the most outlandish stories of my own. When I had them perfected I trotted them out for my father to read. He had taken a course in creative writing at one time and I was sure he knew all about it. He was a reader too. What more does one need to be a critic?

He did his best to critique my stories and to encourage me to continue writing them. Trouble was, he did not believe one could make a living at writing. (In retrospect, I have done everything in my power to prove him right).

More than anything on this earth, I wanted to please my father. I only hope he knew that before he died.

I kept writing only because there was no way for me to stop writing. There was something huge within me that could only be addressed through words. There was a pressure inside that could only be relieved with a pen. I know as little about it now as I did then. It was a metal spring which never seemed to unwind. My tastes in reading were many and varied. I was, in fact, an insatiable reader. It seemed that each time I went to the library a new book or author would reveal itself to me just as I became ready to read such a title. I didn't know how this could be - it was a wonder to me.

When I was still very young I read Hemingway's story 'The Undefeated', and when I had finished I asked my father if the hero had died in the end.

"You're too young to understand that yet," he told me.

Over time I read all of the Hemingways and the Steinbecks and some of the Faulkners, though I found them extremely difficult. Then there was F. Scott Fitzgerald and Jack London (my English teacher was appalled that I should read him), and Joseph Conrad and Robert Louis Stevenson and Graham Greene, who I adored, and James Fennimore Cooper.

Later I discovered Chekhov and Thomas Mann and Kafka and Camus. Henry James and Flaubert and Dostoyevsky. Later still there was Kazantzakis and Borges and Calvino and Celine (now there was a man with a chilling view of the modern landscape), and Hess and D.H. Lawrence.

I was impressed very much by Robert Stone and Peter Matthiessen and Jerzy Kosinski and Truman Capote. I liked, too, Norman Mailer and Henry Miller and Yasunari Kawabata.

Then I found the Latin Americans. How I have loved them. Magic realism is something one can get one's teeth into, I can tell you that much. They were led by Gabriel Garcia Marquez. I read them all. I don't know what to read now.

When my thinking that winter got onto that old course, I should have known I'd be in trouble. There's no going back when you think of the things you've given up over the years. If you get on that old track there's no telling where it will lead. It may take you out beyond where you know yourself, and then you'll get into a horrible mess. Just look at my boss.

Following high school I decided to go on to a trade school. My father was a builder and I wanted more than anything to be

like him. But it was more than that, too. Over the years I had
come to fear insanity with every fiber of my being. Insanity, I
had come to believe, was worse than death. It is like a living
death. And in order to go insane, one had but to cut one's self off
from the real world. One had but to lock one's self in a room and
work out the multitudinous little details of writing a novel and to
forget how to live a day to day life. One had but to let the hedges
grow up around one's existence and live in the darkness, to go
mad. In my mind, it had become that simple.

So the choice was clear. There would be no spookiness for
me. I'd choose a career that would force me out of my own
contemplations and into the real world. Writing was given the
back seat. It was something I could do on the side, for recreation,
when I had nothing better to do. It was something that I would
carefully control, lest it ever try to get away from me.

When I had completed the trade school I joined the army and
was stationed with the 9th Engineer Battalion over in
Aschaffenburg, Germany.

Bound for Germany, I caught a medical flight out of McGuire
Air Force Base. All of the seating on this plane was facing to the
rear and there were only four small round ports for windows. Over
the Atlantic we were engulfed in a tremendous storm. We could
see lightning flashing through the windows and little else. The
fuselage began to shake as fierce winds buffeted us. Then the
plane dropped a hundred feet as if the bottom had fallen out of the
sky. The engines shrieked and strained to regain our lost place in
the air.

Again and again we dropped like an anvil from a balcony but
each time the engines somehow found the ungodly strength to save
us. Once, I thought I heard the anxious laughter of several women,
but there were no women aboard.

Our flight made an unscheduled stop in Lisbon. We waited
several hours while the ground crew went over every inch of the
plane, tightening what had been loosened by the storm. "Jesus
boys," I heard one of them say, "I don't know how this thing
stayed in the air."

Continuing on, I made it safely to Stuttgart, Germany, and
spent a night at the Replacement Station there. Next evening I
boarded a bus headed north to Aschaffenburg. There were thick
banks of fog on each side of the road. At one place, apparently

suspended above us in the fog and darkness, was a castle lighted by fine gold lights. This, truly, was the land of fairy tales.

Many things happened to me in those years, none of which are of particular importance or relevance to what I have to say, but one incident does stand out in my mind as strange as the day it happened:

Our unit had just finished up a field exercise at the training area in Hohenfels. We loaded the trucks and trailers and in the morning we pulled out at about 0 dark thirty, as we always said. It had snowed through the night and the roads were icy and treacherous. We crept along in our vehicles - jeeps, three-quarter-tons, deuce-and-a-halfs, and five-tons.

I was riding shotgun in one of the deuce-and-a-half trucks. We were coming down the back side of a mountain when the jeep in front of us slid on the ice. He spun clear around, trailer and all, and I didn't see how we'd miss him. My driver swore and at the same time steered drastically to the left. There was a dirt road leading off to that side, but we both saw we wouldn't make it. Then there was a short piece of metal guard rail, and then darkness. In the darkness was a drop off a hundred feet deep. The beams of the headlights and our futures were swallowed by this darkness.

With a bravado born of such situations, my driver steered into the guard rail. He clipped the last foot of it. We were sliding on the ice now. The darkness loomed ever closer. I glanced into the mirror on my side. There was a jeep coming up behind us, also sliding on the ice. I knew when he hit us we were going to be pushed right over the edge.

Our truck stopped inches from the cliff. The jeep hit our rear. We didn't budge. I heard the sound of wings in my ears.

"What was that?" my driver said.

"What was what?" I asked.

"What was that sound?"

"I didn't hear anything," I lied.

"It sounded like wings flapping."

"You've got wings flapping in your head," I said playfully. I tousled the boy's hair with my hand. He had saved my life.

Do you believe in the existence of angels? Are they real celestial beings that guard us in our daily lives or are they, perhaps, only symbols that ancient writers employed to explain some higher world. I never used to believe in them...

Anyway, I returned to take a job with that construction company out of Detroit and I had been with them ever since. There was no reason to change anything now. At this point in my life, I had it made. That winter was a long one, though, and I had plenty of time for contemplation. No matter how hard I tried, I couldn't concentrate on my work. Now that the old writing thing had gotten back into my head, there seemed no way to get it out.

I began to read again. I read such diverse works as 'The Unbearable Lightness of Being' by the Czech writer Milan Kundera, and 'Man's Hope' by Andre Malraux, and the short stories of Flannery O'Connor, and 'Darkness At Noon' by Arthur Koestler, and 'Of Human Bondage' by W. Somerset Maugham, and 'The Sailor Who Fell From Grace With The Sea' by Yukio Mishima. Once the floodgates had been opened, there was no stopping the rush of the words that overwhelmed me, nor was there any way to staunch the flow of ideas that began to come into my mind. Soon I was making quick notations on pieces of paper. I made the notes and then folded up the papers and hid them back in my pockets. At night I opened the papers and transcribed what had been scribbled there into my notebook.

Several times that year I contemplated writing a novel myself. But, each time I thought about it, I quickly looked down again. I'd been through all that. Trying to write about modern times is like writing about a maze, I tell you, and who can do that? Besides, I wondered where one found the time for the actual mechanics of writing. With the kind of work I was doing now, I could never find time to write even a short story, let alone a complete novel.

No; better I should keep my head down and work. And so I did. I put the whole business out of my mind. There was no reason giving up all I had worked so hard for over the years just to pursue some foolish youthful dream I had once had. What kind of sense would that make?

Still the ideas flowed into my head and from there I jotted them down on little scraps of paper. There seemed nothing I could do to stop it. Over the next months, as I continued to piece together bits of a story, I came to understand that I could not continue as I had been, no matter what it cost me. I could not continue as a builder. I had resisted my true calling long enough. All of my time and energy had been going into building, which

was something I no longer had any real interest in. I had
somehow overlooked or ignored the only career that would make
me happy - that of being a writer.

In spite of that sudden realization, however, I did not know,
really, where to begin. My frantic scribblings, upon rereading,
proved to be incomprehensible. They were only scattered fragments
of thoughts that never quite added up to make any kind of sense.
Still, I felt the urgent need to break with my old company before
another year passed.

On a Monday morning in late May, I finally screwed up the
courage to turn in my yellow hard hat. This was to the dismay of
one and all. They did like me there, which made it all the tougher.

"What will you do?" they asked. "Where will you go?"

The facts are, I had no idea myself. All I did know was that
my life was constricting me, and that I had become lost in it. If
I was ever going to escape the maze I was trapped in, I would
have to go in search of the something that I now lacked.

THREE

When one makes a sudden break with the past, there follows an extreme sense of vertigo. Where before the feet found a familiar old path worn smooth by many passings, now, in panic, they stumble over unremembered ground. Those who are on even terrain yearn for the unknown, and those who are lost curse the day they left their comfort behind, I suppose.

One of my brothers and I once climbed 14,255 foot Longs Peak in the Colorado Rockies. When we got to the top we fearfully looked over the east face. This east face is a thousand foot drop. We each crept up to the rim and peered over. Having done that, we quickly backed away again and my brother said, "You know, it's not that I'm afraid I'll fall, it's that I don't trust myself - I just might jump!"

That's what vertigo is. It is not only the sensation of falling, or the feeling that one is about to fall, but it is also the very real lack of trust in one's self, being so close to that fateful edge. That, apparently, is what happened to me that year. Being so near the precipice, I had actually become giddy and jumped - forsaking all I had been living for those past ten years. What is more, once I had jumped, I realized only too late, there could be no going back.

Having quit my job, I did not know what I'd do next or where I'd go, as I have already said. I had plenty of money from my savings and from a sizeable severance check the company had issued me, so I didn't have to worry about that. I moved out of my trailer at the construction site and into a hotel room near downtown Kalamazoo. For several weeks I continued my voracious reading campaign, invading the public library and the several local used book stores, hauling off hoards of classics and near classics, and I wandered the streets in the evenings, thinking of the many stories I might one day write. In spite of all that, however, I seemed unable to begin. Every time I wrote those first words I was convinced would throw open the floodgates of my masterpiece, they quickly petered out after only a page or two and I was left

25

with a ream of blank paper staring me in the face, and no inspiration with which to fill them. Worse, I could not even remember why I had begun writing that particular story in the first place, or what I had intended to say in it. As you might imagine, this was quite a painful process.

Perhaps I have not yet established myself very well in the reader's mind. It is far easier to establish one's self as a character in a book than as a real, living, person. The trick is to choose those traits that are solely one's own, and not anyone else's. On the surface that may seem obvious and even simple, but in practice it is rather difficult. What, after all, distinguishes one of us from another?

It may be that I have already painted myself in a certain way, as naive or as predictable or as moody, for instance, when I had no intention of doing so. Like you, reader, I am a many-faceted creature and often a contradictory one driven this way and that by I do not know what forces. But it is entirely possible that I have not completely explained the motives that caused me to change my course in life so abruptly and irrevocably. Let me attempt to do so now:

Ever since I can remember, I have lived a double life. This has not been the cute, fanciful life of a Walter Mitty character, nor the twisted and deranged life of a schizophrenic, but rather the odd, deceptive life of a double agent. As a boy this tendency of mine to infiltrate the lives of others was, I believe, more pronounced. (Perhaps now it has become a permanent part of my nature, and I have learned to accept it). Back then I would go out on secret missions, disguising myself in any way I thought necessary to conceal my true purpose, and then I would probe my quarry for confidential information.

Mostly I wanted to learn about their private lives. I wanted to know what made them the way they were. What skeletons were hidden in their closets. What passions inflamed them.

One neighbor of ours, Mrs. Mattson, wanted to be a country and western singer. Trouble was, she never knew quite how to go about it. Tears came into her wrinkled eyes when she told me.

Mister King was some kind of genius with electricity. He could build a radio with a crystal and some copper wire. He always wore one of those green plastic visors when he worked.

Mister Snow told weird stories about hodags and snow snakes.

I always knew that I would be a writer one day, and that these would be the people I would write about. Once I had obtained their deepest held secrets, I carried them home with me in my memory and there I transcribed them into notebooks. Often I embellished what they told me in the most astonishing ways, a fact of which I am not very proud. (I justified this to myself by saying that I invented what their lives lacked). In this way, as you see, I was able to capture the ideas and dreams, indeed, the very essence of others, and to store them in my secret files.

This was the unknown side of my makeup. The other side, the side I showed the world, was what I now call Mister Pleaser. To conceal the true purpose of my actions, Mister Pleaser was congenial, pleasant, and apparently content. He was the one who got the grades in school, who honored his father and mother, who played sports and participated in student council, and in helping the elderly neighbors shovel their driveways in winter.

Meanwhile my other side continued unsuspected in subversive and covert activities that would shock most people if they heard of them. If you have known me, dear reader, you have known only Mister Pleaser. No one has ever openly met my operative.

Mister Operative, if I may call him that, (in fact he has no name and to name him at all is only an awkward attempt at defining him), acted absolutely without conscience or moral regard. He conducted the most outlandish experiments on his fellows in order to see what the results would be. There was, in his mind, no difference between insect and animal, between animal and human, or between inanimate and animate for that matter. For him, the world was one gigantic laboratory where he had a free hand in conducting his experiments and calculations.

Did you know, as I know from these experiments, that by dripping molten plastic on a cricket you can make it scream like something from a horror movie. It is a strange, nightmarish sound, one that I will never forget. This alternate side of me dissected live frogs and exploded them with firecrackers, and exposed stunned wasps to the concentrated rays of a magnifying glass. He shot small birds with a pellet gun and watched carefully as the little breast breathed its last.

He fed aphrodisiacs that he had concocted with his chemistry set to young girls and then seduced them. (In retrospect I wonder if it was the chemical or only my faith in the chemical that caused my success). By seduction I mean those childish games we have all played in the bushes or as in one case, in an upended rain barrel. This was in the days before I knew anything about the actual act of sex itself.

Only by writing could I ever hope to release the evil pressure that my little dark operative was causing within me. (By writing or by some other form of art, or through obscene criminal activities; I had my choice). He smoldered deep in my soul, never letting me rest. I could act as normally as I wanted during the light of day, but at night I felt him wriggle within me and I knew there was no escape. Long ago he set a time bomb in my psyche, and now it was exploding. That, if it makes any sense, is why I left my good job and set out on this restless adventure in search of the truth about myself. I had to find out, before it was too late, the secret passions of my own life.

Still, at the time I quit, I had no idea at all what I was about. This was an aimless period when one thing had ended and the next had not yet begun. Vertigo set in. I felt like Wile E. Coyote felt each time he shot out over a canyon rim, but before he began to fall. That look of bewilderment; 'How could I have gotten into this spot?' most closely explains how I felt as I hung in time and space, not sure what was yet to come. For all I knew, I was poised over thin air, ready to fall as I had never fallen before.

Then something unexpected happened. (Perhaps anything that happens to a person is unexpected). I went out for a walk one afternoon. The weather was fine and springy. The air was clear and the sun soft and full of good graces. All of the snow had gone some weeks before and we were on for summer. (In Michigan we know how to appreciate spring and summer). While I was out I happened past a travel agency. Actually, I had been by there a hundred times but this time I noticed a large poster in the front window. 'Europe' it read, and there was a photograph of the castle in Heidelberg.

I know what attracted me to that poster, though I am afraid now to say what it was. I was pictured in the photograph. During my tour of duty in Germany I had visited that castle and now there I was featured in a travel poster of the place. Photographic emulsions are simply fascinating to me. If there is magic in this world, emulsions are surely part of it. But (you'll think me odd for sure), when I looked more closely at the poster, it was not me pictured there at all. There was, instead, some short fat German in a hunter's cap. How could I, tall and bearded and with fine Scottish features, have confused myself with this stout jaegermeister? It seemed inconceivable.

An enormous sense of doubt came over me. Was I going mad? Or, perhaps I had only wanted to see myself pictured in that setting. If that was true, and I could discern no other rational explanation, then maybe I should go back overseas and find out what it was all about. Seeing myself pictured in a travel poster might have been a symbol from my unconscious mind - signaling some deep undetected, inner need. I am a man of the twentieth century after all, and am quick to think in those terms. So, whatever the true reason, my curiosity bade me enter the travel agency.

A young lady came right up to me as if she had been expecting me all along. "How nice to see you," she said, "come right in."

This was, for me, a rather unexpected way to be greeted in a place of business. Still, I went in and took the proffered chair.

"Please make yourself comfortable." She had the most striking green eyes and what I can only describe as forward lips. They were lips that imposed themselves on one's territory, and promised more, perhaps, than one should ever hope for.

"I've come about your poster," I blurted abruptly.

"About Europe, you mean," she said, glancing at the front window to see which poster I was speaking of. "You're interested in visiting Europe?"

"I was there before. Once. When I was in the Army." I don't know why I was in such a hurry to explain everything to her.

"I see," she said simply, waiting for me to go on.

Since I had exhausted my fount of ready information in that one spurt, I sat there thickly, waiting for something to happen. In the mean time, I noticed her perfume.

"The reason I was asking," she said at last, to save me from my own lumpishness, "was that I have just returned from there myself. It's such a wonderful place... I really wish I could go back."

"I rather liked it too," I said stuffily, "but I saw most of it from a two-and-a-half-ton truck."

Her eyes positively danced when she spoke, and I found that I was hypnotized by them.

"I absolutely loved it," she said. Those lips. Those lips. I feasted my eyes upon her lips.

"We could go back together," I suggested. (I don't know what possessed me - I am never so bold around women), but there it was out, in spite of me.

She was considering it, I could tell. Her striking eyes were searching my face, gauging the sort of person I really was. 'What are his intentions?' I could hear her asking herself. 'Do I really dare go off on an adventure with a total stranger, no matter how attracted I may be to him?'

For a long moment I had the uncanny feeling that she was going to accept my unexpected invitation. Then with a certain smile on her lips she turned to get a book from the shelf behind her. Just as she reached for the book, however, the entire shelf fell with a bang and the poor girl jumped back, startled out of her wits. The books from the shelf cascaded down onto the floor with a tremendous noise.

"I didn't do anything," she said, turning first to look at me, and then at the others in the office. "I didn't even touch it." Then, with an escalating panic; "I don't know why this always has to happen to me."

Having lost her composure so completely, the girl began to cry. "Nothing ever works out for me," she said through her tears. "I've had such a rotten day."

Two other women were in the office at the time. Both of them were older by ten years than this girl. When they saw that she was now crying uncontrollably, they both came over in a hurry and gave me a hell of a look.

I wanted to explain that it had not been my fault, but there seemed to be no way for me to do this. I was as bewildered by what happened as anyone.

"The book shelf fell..." I began lamely. When I said it, I understood just how silly it sounded.

"It's true," the girl said through her tears. Her mascara had run in long streaks down her face. The other two women were applying tissues. It was clear they did not know what to think about all this. One of them was probably the owner of the agency.

"I'm sorry," the girl sobbed. "I don't know why I'm making such a fuss. I must look really stupid."

"There, there," one of the women said.

"I'm new here, you see," the girl told me. "I'm new to this town and to this job." She was regaining her composure. Now she had the hiccups. Horrible, painful ones.

"I understand," I said.

"I've been trying to do the best job I know how only, I keep having trouble. I don't know why."

Sitting there, I must have looked thoroughly overwhelmed and distressed, (which indeed, I was), for one of the women, probably the owner, turned to me with her kindest, most apologetic face and said, "Could I help you book your tour or your flight or whatever..."

"That's very kind," I said, "but I'm in no hurry. If it's alright, I'd like to have this young lady help me."

"Oh that's quite alright," she said uncertainly, as if she was not at all sure it was alright. (What is the protocol for such a situation, after all?) "I only meant that if you were pressed for time..."

"Not in the least," I assured her.

She gave me a bemused look, and then turned back to the girl. The other woman's ministrations had saved the girl from her embarrassment now and we were soon able to get back to the business at hand. This began, however, only after profuse apologies from the girl.

"About that trip..." I said, trying to force her back onto the proper track.

"I'm very sorry, I was about to tell you, there is really no way for me to go with you. You ought to have a marvelous time, though." A certain caginess had come into her green eyes.

"Of course," I said, accepting the sudden change in her tone. "I imagine I will have a good time."

"We've just gotten word about some really low fares to London..."

"That would be great," I said. The moment was past for the two of us.

I booked the flight and on the way home bought bus tickets to New York City. I tried to act normally but I had the most peculiar feeling about the way my life had been going lately. It was as if my secret operative had taken wings and was now somehow manipulating the way things were working out. I know that's not possible, of course, but something strange was surely happening. That incident with the shelf of books falling at the most inopportune moment, and then the poor girl's violent reaction to it was all positively perplexing, and more than a little disconcerting. Still, I was able to put all that out of my mind soon enough. I had a trip to plan.

Travel will take you out of yourself quicker than anything, I've found. It breaks all your little routines at once and sets your whole life on edge. Even the mere idea of going somewhere stimulates a sense of anticipation and images of strange and exotic doings form inside the brain like emulsions in a darkroom.

I left Kalamazoo by bus on the fifth of June that year. With me I took a backpack full of clothes and camping gear and maps, and a sleeping bag. That way I'd be ready for whatever mode of travel presented itself to me, and no matter what accommodations.

Next day I arrived in New York City. We came down through the Holland Tunnel with its glazed bricks that seemed close enough on my side to reach out and touch. I was bleary-eyed by then, having come straight through on the bus as I had. The trip had taken eighteen hours and during the night we had passed through or stopped at any number of little mountain coal towns in Pennsylvania. My eyelids felt gummy. I had dozed off between stops but the air in the bus was so stale and smokey that I felt as if I had not slept at all. Before I headed out of the station, I stowed my backpack in a locker. The metal frame of the pack would not fit, so I was forced to carry that with me.

Now, as I came out of the Port Authority Station, I felt suddenly alive again, renewed by my own sense of what lay ahead. Things were moving again. Traffic and people were flowing back and forth. There was noise and plenty of it. My blood began running. I followed the flow of the crowd along, just to see where it would take me. Surprisingly, it led me down into the Bowery.

Because my flight would not depart JFK until the next noon, I had decided to let Rozinante have her head. I dropped her reigns and now she had led me Quixote-fashion, here to the old Belltone

Hotel. The front of the place was grim. Inside, I was confronted by an unshaven fifty year old man inside a wire cage.

"Ten bucks a night," he growled. Then, eye-balling me up and down, "Take your own chances."

"That's the first time anyone has ever told me a thing like that," I said with a smile.

He grunted, but did not say more. He took my ten dollars and pointed at a water-stained old registration book. I signed my name and accepted the key that was hung on a smooth plastic spindle. Then, before going upstairs, I went back through a low-ceilinged hall and entered the day room.

There it seemed I had entered another world. Along the wall to my left four men were hunkered down with their backs to the wall. Each was in a different stage of roping off his arm with a rubber hose, torching some heroin in a spoon, drawing it into a syringe, and, holding the rubber tubing taut in their teeth, pushing the needle into a ready vein. Then, one by one, they fell back against the wall and slid to the floor in animated postures of relief.

One of the men looked over at me with dazed eyes and said, "Hey, is that your old lady?"

"Who?" I said, glancing over my shoulder. It made me nervous to have been picked out like that.

The man did not answer. His eyes closed and his head lolled back against the wall.

There were others in the room. Puerto Ricans and blacks and a few seedy-looking white guys. The place was hot and stuffy. Everything had a musty smell. One of the blacks got out of his chair and ambled up to me. "Man," he said, "you got five dollar'?"

"No," I told him.

He eyed me suspiciously. "My name's Grady. What's yours?"

I told him.

"You educated, ain't you?"

"I guess I am."

"Why you ain't got five dolla'?"

"I'm on my way home," I lied smoothly. "I was in the army. I got out. Now I'm headed home."

"They don't give you no money when you get out?"

"I sent it home. All I've got is bus tickets. I'll be leaving in the morning."

"That so?"

"Yes," I said, "that is so."

"What's that?" He pointed at the frame from my backpack. "That your chair? You don't need to carry your chair around with you. Nobody ain't going to steal your chair."

"You're probably right," I said with a shrug. I carried it up to my room. Grady followed me up on the old wooden elevator. When I had stashed the thing under my bed, I turned back to the door. Grady was looking in from behind me.

When I came out he said, "Come on, man. I gotta' get some bread somewhere."

"Where are we going?" I began to sweat.

"Around, man. We're goin' to go around different places." I noticed that Grady was trembling slightly and sweat was trickling down his face.

We went back to the dayroom. He began talking to some of the guys in there. They were making some kind of deal, apparently. Then a Cuban with a wicked face came in. He was not big but he was carrying a baseball bat. "Where's Jose?" he said. "I heard Jose been selling the stuff down here."

"Go on, man," Grady said. "He ain't been around here."

"You see him, you tell him I goin' fix his ass."

"Yeah, alright. But he ain't around."

The Cuban left. Grady turned to me. "That' hotel security, man. Sorry piece of shit." Then, after grinning for another moment, "Come on, man."

We headed out the door and onto the street.

"Where we going?" I asked again.

"We gotta' score 'fore that asshole rent-a-cop screws everything up around here."

Grady was sidling along, walking nearly sideways as if trying to keep his back to the wall. We went into a nearby department store. There, before I knew what any of this was going to be about, he swiped two new white dress shirts. I didn't know what was going to happen next. Would he be caught? Would they arrest me along with him? He had whipped the shirts up under his own shirt so fast I hadn't had time to adjust to the idea. I began to panic.

"Be cool," Grady said.

I didn't trust myself to say anything. I thought I was going to go in my pants. There was a store clerk just behind us. Surely he had seen what was going on. He began to say something to us. Then I heard the sound of wings flapping just behind me and I nearly passed out.

Grady had half a smile on his face. He seemed to be enjoying this about as much as I was not. Still smiling, he eased his way out of the store. I followed along, numb with fear.

I breathed easier once we were back outside. "Now where are we going?" I asked, still tagging along after him.

"We got to go over to Port Authority, man. We got to sell these here shirts."

He led the way down into the bowels of the huge bus station and he sold the shirts to one of the drivers for five dollars. Five dollars was the magic number for him. He went out on the street and scored a fix.

I didn't sleep well that night. The air in the room was hot and sticky and the mattress on the bed was mushy. Noise came up from the streets like I was sleeping in a construction site. I tipped the wooden chair up and slid it under the knob of my door. Then I lay there wondering why I had undertaken such an adventure as this.

During the night someone tried the knob but, finding the door secured, moved on.

In the morning I tried to slip away but Grady caught me out on the sidewalk. "Where you goin'?" he called.

"I gotta' catch the bus," I said. "I'm headed home, I told you that."

"Oh, yeah. I see you got your chair with you."

"That's right."

"Give me five dollar', man." He came over and stood so close that I had to look into his eyes. He looked dangerous, and in serious need of a fix. Without further hesitation I reached into my pocket and pulled out a five dollar bill.

"That's 'a way, baby," he said. Five dollars was the magic number for Grady. He'd gotten it early today and without a fight.

"That's the last I've got," I promised.

"Thanks, man. It's what I needed."

"Alright," I said, and headed up the street to the bus station.

FOUR

As soon as my plane was out over the Atlantic I had the distinct impression that everything I remembered about my stay in New York had occurred a long time ago, and in some illusory dream. Why had I gone to the Bowery in the first place? I wondered. It had never been my intention to spend any time there. What had been the big attraction? What had lured me into those mean streets? The whole affair had been foolish and dangerous, especially considering the fact that one mishap could have ruined my entire trip.

My plans had taken a life of their own, it seemed. Though I planned one thing, my intentions somehow became tangled and I ended up doing something entirely different. Ever since I had decided to change the course of my life, destiny had taken control and there was nothing more I could do about it.

In the beginning I had been the quintessential modern man, I know that now. I had been helpless and bored and restless and trapped in the maze that is modern existence. My future had been bleak - the never-ending chore of living unwound itself out of control toward the horizon of my days. I felt useless. My life had become a marionette that was manipulated by one and all except me. I had always done things to please others, but had never done anything to please myself. And, if this is not my life to lead, whose is it?

Because I had made the decision to leave that kind of life behind, the various twists and turns in events had somehow led me to the Bowery. It was incomprehensible to me how this had happened. Once there, I had witnessed an entire civilization of people who were lost. These were people who had succumbed to various modern maladies, and had become confused and turned around and lost in the maze, just as might have happened to me had I stayed where I was, in my former life.

But now that I had escaped 'that' maze, was I not only trapped in another kind of maze? This was the question that unsettled me as we flew over the Atlantic that day.

A steward came along the aisle dressed in a white linen suit which was a sharp contrast to the way people had dressed in the Bowery, needless to say. "Any wine?" he asked, pouring as he went. My life was back in first class, at least.

I took a glass of the white wine and sipped it quietly as we continued on toward the British Isles. A sudden storm had backed air traffic up at Heathrow so we were diverted to Stansted, which lies further to the north. From there we were bussed through the misty English countryside to the edge of London. We were left at King's Cross. It had grown dark already, and since I had no idea where else to go, I decided to stay right there. On the corner was a small bed and breakfast hotel, the Morgan Court, so I checked in.

It was run by a quiet little fellow from India who asked in a friendly way where I was from.

"I'm American," I explained.

"Yes," he said patiently, "but from which place, please?"

I mentioned Kalamazoo and then Detroit, but he had heard of neither of these. Then I tried Michigan.

"I'm so sorry, is this place near Chicago maybe?"

"Why yes," I said, "it is. I live not far from Chicago."

"Ah, that is very good," he said. "Chicago, Michigan."

That night I dreamed I was negotiating a jungle river. There was no way to see what lay around each new bend ahead. Because I did not know what was there, I was fearful.

I wanted to wake up. To call out. But I could not pull myself up from the muck of my dream. I was afraid because I could not understand the interconnectedness of the river and its tributaries without the proper perspective.

Do you believe that dreams are an experience from another dimension that we can access, perhaps, only in our sleep, or are they simply the inner workings of our complex minds?

In the morning I headed out into the gorgeous clear day and started into town. My Indian friend had given me general directions to Victoria Station, but advised I take a cab instead of walking. But the day was too wonderful for a taxi and I was in no particular hurry anyway. That was a good thing, as it turned out.

"For the train to the south you will be needing Victoria Station, I'm afraid. That is a very long walk from here," my hotel friend informed me. "But if you must walk, please keep to the south. It is south even of Buckingham Palace on Buckingham Palace Road, I believe."

Without a care in the world I set out down King's Cross Road and then turned onto Guilford Street which led me across to Southampton Row and the British Museum, a monumental building in the Greek style, and from there up Oxford. Somewhere along there I should have turned south, just as my friend had advised me, perhaps on Charing Cross Road, but for some reason I persisted westward to Bayswater Road and Hyde Park. There, in the park, (I thought I might cut through to the south), I was accosted by a grizzled old bum who had slept the night there under a tall tree, and was now drinking his breakfast from a bottle of wine.

"Where are you going?" he said.

"I don't know," I said.

"How are you going to get there if you don't know where it's at?" he said.

"Good question."

"You could always stay right here."

"I don't think so," I said.

"It's not so bad."

"I'm just passing through."

"Could you spare a quid for a fellow traveler?"

"I don't even know what that is."

"A pound sterling, old boy. Or, if you haven't got that, just something to help me through the day. I don't require much, you know."

I gave him a dollar. I had not yet exchanged any money, I realized.

"Bless you. Please, ask me anything."

"Can you give me directions to Victoria Station?"

His eyes went vacant. "Sure," he said feebly. "It's... just... that way." He pointed south.

Keeping to the south I crossed over the Serpentine on West Carriage Drive, but then was lured into Kensington Gardens by my own curiosity. There I became turned around again and was emitted, eventually, on Bayswater Road. I stopped a man on the street and asked him the way to Victoria Station but he only laughed and pointed far to the southeast.

I turned south, again, on Kensington Palace Gardens but then got myself off track and somehow found myself on Kensington Church Street which ran down toward the huge Royal Garden Hotel. Along here there were many little shops and I stopped in at one to ask directions.

The shop was full of every kind of antique and collectible, from china and crystal to Japanese swords and armor. Here, truly, were items from all over the world. I was so overwhelmed by the variety of goods around me that I nearly forgot what I had come in for.

Off in the corner to my left the owner of the shop smiled and came in my direction. "How may I be of service to you this fine morning?" he asked. His voice had something of an English accent, but also something else.

"I'm sorry," I said, "I was just looking."

"No need to apologize for that," he said. He had a hale and hearty manner.

"Well, actually, I am looking for Victoria Station. I thought I'd stop in and ask directions, if you don't mind."

"I don't mind at all," he said. "I wonder, though, have we met somewhere before? You seem very familiar to me."

"This is my first time in London."

"That must be true," he said. Then, by way of explaining himself, "Since you don't know where Victoria Station is located."

"Unless you've been to Kalamazoo, Michigan, you've probably never met me," I said.

"I've not been there, and that's a fact. Tell me, what is your name?"

I told him.

"Mine's Daniel Allman. I travel all over the world in this business, as you might imagine. You never know when our paths might have crossed."

"I have never traveled much," I said. "I did spend some time in Germany..."

"Well, perhaps our paths will cross again someday. One never knows."

"That's true," I said seriously, "one never knows." Of course I thought this exchange was a little curious then, not knowing what I now know about the interconnectedness of all things. I did not, then, see how it was possible we should ever meet again.

He was a man perhaps a few years older than myself and, as he drew near, I noticed that he had a peculiar oriental cast to his features - especially his eyes, which slanted away from the center of his face in mild surprise. "I could give you directions, to be sure, or I could do you one better than that."

"In what way?" I said.

"I know of a man going in that direction. If you'd care to wait a few minutes, I'm quite sure he'd be happy to have you along."

I was a little surprised by this coincidence. "You mean to tell me that someone from here is going to Victoria Station?"

"That's exactly what I mean to say."

"But..." I looked around in an animated way, "who?" This was some kind of subtle joke, I was sure.

He could see the look of doubt in my face. "He is a teacher, a good friend of mine. He is going over to the Continent to travel around a bit, and to visit Paris, where he keeps an office."

"I see," said I, not wanting to fall for something foolish. After all, I didn't know anyone here, and so could trust no one. "Perhaps if you could give me directions..."

"Nonsense," a man called as he came out from a back room. He was a short man, carrying a suitcase with him. "I heard the last of your conversation and I will be most happy to take you to Victoria Station. My name is Frederich Nagel and I am at your service."

In the semi-darkness of the place it was impossible to make him out clearly. His voice had a certain Germanic sound to it. "I don't know..." I said at last.

"If you're lost, I know the way," he assured me.

"Are you going to the station?" I asked, just to be sure I was clear about that.

"Yes, of course. My car is waiting out on the street if you care to join me."

He came out into the open light from the front window now and I must have looked truly surprised. "But you... you..."

"Yes, what is it?"

"I saw your picture on a poster back in the States. You were standing next to the Heidelberg Castle." My head was reeling with this realization now.

"That may very well be true."

"Then it was you..."

"I don't deny it is possible."

"But," I stammered, "you don't understand. That was the very poster that inclined me to go into the travel agency and then, once I was in there, to..." The implications of my thoughts were simply too large for me to comprehend.

"Perhaps it is you who does not understand," the teacher said. "The world is full of many strange and wondrous things."

"Are you German?" I asked, not knowing quite what to say.

"I am Swiss," he said, "of German and Austrian decent."

"And you have been to Heidelberg?" I was still trying to grasp the immensity of the thing that had happened. I mean, what is the probability that one will meet, in a shop in London, the very man one saw in a travel poster in Kalamazoo?

"Of course I have been there. How else could my picture appear in a poster?"

"Then it is true; it was you. I can't believe it. You see, when I first looked at the poster, I thought I saw myself pictured there. It seems so strange now. That is what caused me to stop and take a closer look."

Had I, then, been lured here by some mystical force I did not understand?

"I can hardly be held responsible for that," the short man said.

"No, I suppose not. Still, it is fascinating, don't you think?" I was becoming more and more incredulous by the moment. This line of reasoning was too much for me. I have always been a practical man, at least until I quit my perfectly good construction job. There has never been any reason for me to go seeking truths that are beyond the physical realm. What is real, to my mid-western upbringing, is what I can grasp in my two hands. If there is anything beyond that, I don't care to know about it.

Such were my thoughts at that moment.

"Are you alright, Sir?" the shop owner, Allman, asked me.

"Tsch, tsch." The other man made that particular noise with his tongue. "This poor man... I don't even know his name..."

"Sanderson. His name is Sanderson, Sir."

"This man, Sanderson, has come a very long way to be here and is apparently being confronted with issues he has never even considered before. It is our task to help him see what he has been missing."

"Missing?" I interrupted. "I don't feel I've been missing anything." I had suddenly come back to my senses.

"I was speaking about truths..."

"I'm a Methodist," I said. "That's all I need to know."

"Yes, I see," the teacher said. "You like to take the methodical way to truth."

"That's absolutely right," I agreed. "I know how things are and you aren't going to knock me off my feet with a simple trick."

"Oh I assure you, Mister Sanderson, this is no trick," Allman said. "You see, I am a very recent initiate to all this myself. But once you have begun, you will find that there is no going back."

"That is exactly right," the other man, Nagel, said.

"Once I have begun what? I don't intend to begin anything. The only thing I'm going to begin is my trip out of here."

"Oh, but you already have begun your trip," the teacher said.

I gave a nervous little laugh. "This is some kind of trap, isn't it?"

"Not at all," the older man said. "The trap is what you have just broken out of. Now you can begin to understand yourself, and the world you live in."

"Who are you people?" I demanded. "Why are you acting so strangely. What is this all about?"

"Ah, the questions have begun already," Nagel said. "If you have a few moments, my friend, I will explain everything. I will be happy to take you to the train station any time you wish. You have plenty of time. If you would only listen to what I have to say."

"It doesn't hurt anything to listen," I said, setting my jaw stubbornly. Still, I did feel some danger in being there. This was all some elaborate scheme, I was sure, though I could not see why they had perpetrated it, nor to what end. I certainly did not trust them.

"Let me begin by saying that no meeting between two people ever occurs by accident. That being true, in short, we have all come a long way to be here."

"And for what purpose?" I demanded.

"Well, that is the question, isn't it? I am a teacher. Perhaps you have come to learn."

"Perhaps," I said.

"There is an old saying; 'when one is ready, the teacher will come.' I am the teacher. I wonder, are you ready to learn?"

"I don't know," I admitted. A strange feeling of warmth was coming over me. I wondered if I was being hypnotized by his words. Where before I had felt balky, suddenly I felt I truly understood the words he spoke, and that his teachings would not harm me. Without warning, I had begun to trust this gentle man. Then I snapped myself out of it.

"What is this?" I growled.

"Please," he said, "I have a story to tell you. Then if you find you still distrust me, you may go. My car will take you to the station if you wish. Is that fair?"

"Go ahead and tell your story," I said. Once again I was rebelling. Even if I did have something to learn from this man, there was no time in which to learn it. Soon I would be on my way over the channel and probably I would never see these people again.

"This is a story told to me by an old woman in Korea. It is, how shall I say, very appropriate to your situation, I think."

"How do you know anything about me?" I objected.

The older man held up his hand. "Please. You are here. That alone says volumes."

"Herr Nagel is the leader of Paragon," Daniel Allman interjected. "Paragon is one of the great undertakings of mankind."

"Let's not get ahead of ourselves," the teacher cautioned.

I was looking at Mister Allman. I wondered what he had meant by that.

"The story I was told goes as follows: There was a rat caught in a maze. He could not find his way out. At each turning he became more and more confused. The walls of the maze, however, were made of rice paper. At any moment, if the rat had known to gnaw through the rice paper, he could have been free. But he did not know the walls of the maze were made of rice paper, so he continued through the maze as if the walls were made of stone. But for the rice paper, which could easily have been broken through, he was free. Instead, he lived his life as a prisoner. Does this story make sense to you, Sir?"

I nodded, still mulling over what had been said. "The maze itself was an illusion, is that it. The rat was deceived by the illusion, so he was held prisoner in the maze by his own lack of perception."

"Have you not been a rat in a rice paper maze yourself? Have you not somehow broken through the rice paper. Is that not why you are here?"

"Yes," I whispered in spite of myself. In searching, I had come to find something extraordinary. That much I now understood.

"So you understand only too well the meaning of this story and why you have come here."

I nodded again.

"But now that you have broken out of the first maze, you find yourself caught in another maze, is that correct. Your work is not yet done. You have, in fact, only begun."

"I still don't understand how you can know so much about me."

"There is not so much to understand as you might think my friend. Once you have stepped outside all of the various mazes that humankind finds itself trapped in, you will very easily see how others are caught, though the walls of their prisons are made of rice paper."

"This is what you teach?" I asked, turning suddenly to face the old man.

"This is what is called enlightenment," he said. "I teach that one may understand one's self."

"I want to learn," I said, even before I was aware of what I was saying. Some deep need in me was speaking.

"Very good," the teacher said. "That is very good indeed."

Why had I made this sudden change toward these men when only moments before I had been so distrustful. Perhaps I had become entranced by his voice and his alive, penetrating eyes, but I now believe I was entranced by my own need to learn. This, after all, was why I had left my job and my home and had come in search of something I did not know already. Is that not why one travels?

"I just want to know what there is to know," I said at last. "I want to find out what has been missing in my life."

"Welcome to Paragon," the shop owner said.

"What is that?" I said. "I heard you mention that before. Is that some kind of club or something?"

The older man laughed. "There is plenty of time to explain all that later. I'm afraid there is not time now. Would you like me to take you to Victoria Station?"

"But, I don't understand... I thought I would be staying with you. I thought I would be learning from you."

"Perhaps we could travel a way together," he said kindly.

I thought this over for a moment and then said, "I was told I could catch a ferry in Harwich. The train from Victoria Station will take me there, won't it?"

"So it will," Allman said.

"I too am going across," Herr Nagel said. "Since you are ready to begin, I will go that way with you. At some point I can break off, and go on to Paris."

"I really haven't made set plans for my travels," I explained. "Everything was left open. I can go any way I can find."

"That is the only way to travel," Herr Nagel said. "You yourself can never make your own plans. All arrangements have already been made for you."

"That sounds mysterious," I said.

"Oh, not at all. When you begin to study the way of things, you will see soon enough what I mean."

I was becoming more intrigued by the minute. Something quite extraordinary was happening to me, and I was ready for it to happen.

We bade goodbye to Mr. Allman and, picking up our bags, we headed back out into the day. A car was waiting, just as he had promised, and we were driven straight away to Victoria Station. There, I bought a ticket for Harwich, which is on the coast.

FIVE

The trouble with writing about real life, I have found, is that the story always seems to be getting ahead of itself. Real life waits for no one and it certainly does not wait for explanations to be all neatly printed out on a white page. If only it did! Then the whole of our days could be spent in the past, and we could lavish each minute with reason, order, and purpose. As it is, however, we are always breathlessly trying to catch up with the scene that is whizzing by at every turn. How are we supposed to figure out what's going on when it's impossible to freeze the picture for even a second?

When I review what I have written thus far, I find that I have neglected to tell many important things, but that the telling of them would interrupt the natural flow and pace of actual events. This leaves me in a quandary, as you might well imagine. I should write, for instance, that I do not now believe the German fellow pictured in that travel poster back in Kalamazoo was in fact the same man I met there in a London curiosity shop. No, somehow my mind had filled in the gaps left in my memory and I only supposed them to be one and the same. Still, it is interesting that I should have been so quick to believe such a coincidence, don't you agree?

I do not consider myself to be thick-headed or dull. Who does? But I was so quickly taken in by this pair that I am now surprised by my own gullibility. They could have been anyone, after all, even hardened criminals. My desire to experience the world and to learn from it, I believe, led me to act differently than I might normally have acted. Normally, I should say I am a prudent fellow.

But the deed was done, I had made my choice, and I was on my way across the English countryside with this older gentleman; this self-styled teacher. All along the way I kept trying to convince myself that I was only buddying up with him for convenience's sake. After all, what could I really hope to learn from this old guy that I didn't already know myself? He had told me one little story about the rat and the rice paper but that was it. Since then he hadn't said three words to me. Time was going by and before we knew it he was going to be off to Paris and I'd be on my own again, none the smarter for the trip.

Still, there didn't seem to be any harm in traveling along with him for a few miles. Perhaps he badly needed the company.

Looking at him now, I noticed that his hair had grown very thin on top and that little white flecks of dandruff clung in it here and there. He might be older than I had at first thought. His head was large and round and there were several rolls of fat on the back of his neck above his shirt collar. His eyes were the merest blue - so pale as to remind me of a wolf's eyes, and they were still as glass. He was wearing a grey suit, white shirt, and a deep blue tie. In the luggage rack overhead he had placed a single carriage bag, which I could only assume contained all of his travel gear.

Others on the train were boisterous, there were British soldiers playing cards and drinking beer up the car from us, but we sat quietly. I was somewhat startled, in fact, when at last he turned to me and handed me a printed business card. "Won't you take my card," he said, "in the event that we ever become separated."

"Why would we ever become separated?" I asked. I took the card and looked at it. It was white card stock with raised black lettering.

"One never knows," he said. "Besides, I think we may be going separate ways soon."

"What makes you think that?"

He looked at me closely. "What do you think of angels?" he said.

"What do I think of what?" I asked in surprise. I had heard what he said well enough, but his question was so unexpected I needed a moment to consider it.

"Angels. Do you believe they exist?"

"I've never thought much about it," I said. "Why do you ask?"

He continued to look at me evenly, a slight smile on his lips, and said, "There seems to be one nearby."

In spite of myself I glanced over my shoulder, but could see no one. Then, realizing that he was pulling my leg, I turned back and laughed in his face. "That's very funny," I exclaimed.

"Is it," he said mildly. "In what way?"

"Even if there were angels, and I don't really believe there
are, we mortals certainly would not be able to see them."

"Why not?"

He seemed so earnest that I answered, "Because they're
heavenly. They're not of this earth. Besides, why would one ever
even want to come here?"

"That's a good question," he said. A thoughtful look came
over his face.

His serious expression made me want to laugh again, to prove
that he couldn't trick me so easily, and yet I was not quite certain
that he was joking. I had just met the old boy, after all, and I
didn't know what to make of him. Perhaps he actually was
considering the existence of angels. If that was true, though, it
could mean only one thing - he was simply another eccentric old
fool in a world full of fools.

That would explain a great deal, I realized. Here was
somebody's odd old grandpa, (Daniel Allman's?), that they had
managed to unload on an unsuspecting American tourist for a
while. The fact that the old guy believed he was some kind of
spiritual teacher didn't hurt, either. There was always some naive
traveler like me about, seeking truth. Well here it was alright - the
whole truth, staring me straight in the face: either this was some
elaborate hoax, or I was baby-sitting somebody's bumbling old
grandparent.

"Why do you suppose an angel would be here?" I asked him.
Turnabout is fair play, as they say.

"I was just thinking about that," he said.

"Yes, and what did you decide?"

"Angels shuttle back and forth to earth quite regularly, I
believe, but for one to become of this world, some mistake must
have been made."

"A mistake. Then by that you mean to say that mistakes can
be made in heaven."

"Not in heaven," he said quietly. "Here on earth. The
angelic is something between heaven and earth, is it not? And so,
it is possible for an angel to get turned around and end up here on
earth, rather than in heaven."

This was becoming somewhat exasperating for me. More so,
I believe, since his reasoning made a certain kind of sense. That
is to say, it would have made sense if there were, in fact, angels.

My religious training does not prohibit the existence of angels, of course, but I always had the idea they were some sort of metaphor used to argue the existence of heavenly wonders. For me to accept them as real, it would be necessary for me to meet one face to face. I am a practical, and that is to say a skeptical man.

"Do you have nothing further to say on the subject?" the old man inquired.

"I'm speechless," I admitted.

"Heavenly wonders often leave us speechless," he said with a nod of his fat head.

We rode along in silence for some time. In spite of myself I continued to mull over what he had said. Then, between thoughts, I chastised myself for considering seriously anything the old fool had said. 'There's nothing to it,' I'd scoff inwardly. 'Put it out of your head.' But it was not that simple.

The pastor of the church I grew up in, recently retired, was a pragmatic man. He was a man after my own heart, in fact. He was a scholarly man who weighed every argument carefully. There was no room in his heart for mystical experiences, it was quite clear. Each argument and each fact had to be studied and pondered before a final statement could be made on any subject. He was the most knowledgeable man I have ever met.

What would he make of this angel argument, I wondered. Probably he would dismiss the whole thing out of hand, having dealt with it on one level or another at some time in the distant past. "Angels are the fabrications of our dreams," he would say. "At best they are the messengers of man's own psyche. At worst they are scapegoats for man's determination to do what man will do." Such would most likely be his position on angels.

Still, neither his considered position nor old Frederich Nagel's wild speculations represented my thinking in this matter. The fact was, I did not know where I stood on the subject, and that is what led to my long silent ponderings that day.

If there were angels, and that was a big 'if' for me, what would they look like and what would be their true place in heaven and on earth? Would they be men or women or both? Would they have earthly bodies or heavenly? From my studies, the material on this subject, both biblical and otherwise, is rather sketchy. Facts are, nobody really seems to know much about them.

Based upon this lack of information, then, I think it is safe to reject the existence of angels altogether. Surely there are more photographs and reported sightings of UFO's than of angels. One would be more likely, in that case, to spot an alien than an angel, and I'm not holding my breath waiting for that to happen either. This, of course, is assuming that one does not hold them as being both the same.

No, spending so much time considering angels is only a preposterous waste and I would have thought nothing more about it except for what was to happen a short while later.

I turned to Herr Nagel but he was preoccupied with thoughts of his own, and was gazing out the window at the bright countryside. To attract his attention it would have been necessary to tap his shoulder or in some other way to jostle him. What I had to say, a refutation of his angel nonsense, was not really worth saying. From then on I decided to put the whole thing out of my mind.

As a matter of fact, I decided to slip away from the old man at my first opportunity once we had reached Harwich. How had I become saddled with him in the first place? Next thing he would be telling me that he was an angel himself! Such is the nonsense one runs into when traveling.

"We'll be in Harwich soon," Herr Nagel said, turning suddenly to search my eyes with his own.

"Yes," I said nonchalantly, "we will." I wondered if he could see my secret intentions with his piercing eyes of a hunter.

"Have we learned anything from one another, my friend?" He said 'Freund' in the German way.

"I know I have," I said facetiously.

"There is more yet to learn," he said half under his breath.

I had heard him very well and yet I asked, "What was that?" Perhaps I only wanted clarification.

"One can only learn through experience."

"What is that supposed to mean?"

"This talk of angels is quite useless. Only through direct experience, through struggle, through confrontation, can we hope really to understand a thing."

"If I didn't know better, Sir, I would say you are expecting me to meet a real angel at any time."

Again he was piercing me with his predatory eyes. "But," he objected, "that would be ridiculous, would it not?"

I grinned. "I should say it would be, Sir." Had I, then, gained a small victory for Truth?

"There is no need to call me sir. You feel no real respect for me, so why use that word. Is it only because I am older than you that you call me sir?"

How could I respond to that? I wondered. Indeed, I felt cornered now. He had discovered my private ridicule and this made me feel ashamed. Much better, now, to slip away and be done with all this. I needed to circumvent the truth to save face: "I call anyone I scarcely know sir, as a matter of fact. It has no real meaning of any kind. It is only a manner of speaking."

"I see," he said. A hard smile came to his face. Hard and knowing.

We came into Harwich now. Out on the station platform I immediately went into the little act I had been rehearsing in my mind. "I need to find a post office..."

"Going to send a letter home are you?" Herr Nagel said, raising an eyebrow.

"That's right. Where can I meet up with you again?"

"At the ferry?" he said.

"Good idea." I glanced at my watch. Even going through the motions, though, I had the idea he was on to my little deception. We made arrangements to meet at the ferry before its departure later that evening, but he seemed to have no particular interest in these plans.

That afternoon I passed the time exploring the docks and later, at about the time the ferry left with Herr Nagel aboard, I took a room and spent the night.

The next morning was foggy. By about ten, however, the fog had burned off and I went down to the ferry to check my baggage and to make arrangements for the crossing. Oddly, I felt a sense of loneliness without the old guy around. In a way I had been looking forward to traveling with him and learning from him. Perhaps I should have stuck with him in spite of his queer nature. At least I could have learned something from him; his past, his one-time aspirations, his lost loves and dreams and such. Now, as it was, I had no one.

This was even more true than I would like to admit. During high school I had dated a couple of girls but nothing had ever come of it. With them, there had never been any spark. The dates were complete disasters. We couldn't talk to each other. We couldn't laugh. There was nothing tender between us and absolutely nothing to look forward to. After a few dates like these, fiascos each of them, I gave up on the idea of ever meeting the right girl. I'm the kind of person who would have to be swept off my feet, I guess, and that simply never happened.

All of my high school chums had either gotten married or moved away and my brothers had gone on to lives of their own. The sad truth is I had grown rather used to being alone. This was not by choice so much as it was, I suppose, by predisposition. Though I had grown accustomed to being alone, I had never grown used to loneliness. It went with me everywhere like a haunting melody.

That night I crossed the channel to Hook van Holland. There was a big moon and I stayed out on the rail looking into the dark deep waters until late. Then I went to my cabin and slept until morning.

The morning was cold and foggy. I had left my jacket in my backpack so the first thing I wanted to do was claim my baggage. The short-sleeved shirt I was wearing did little to keep out the dampness. Unhappily, my baggage was not there. The man behind the window wondered if I might check back in an hour. His English was broken. I had no Dutch.

An hour later it had not come in. An hour after that and it had still not come in. The man sent a telegram back to England. The return telegram said that they would try to find the baggage and have it on the ferry next morning. The day cleared some. There was nothing to do but wait.

I went to a bank and changed some travelers checks. After that I walked around town an hour or so and then I stopped in at a little restaurant for lunch. There was a girl at one of the tables. She looked up when I came in.

"Hello," I said, taking a table near hers.

"Hello," she said.

"You're American," I said.

"Yes." She smiled weakly.

"You don't sound very sure of it," I laughed.

"I'm American," she said, putting more certainty in her voice.

By the look of her she had been traveling long and hard. On the floor next to her table there was a backpack and some sort of floppy hat. She was wearing hiking boots, I noticed.

"Have you been traveling long?"

"Oh yes," she said quickly. "I've come far."

I waited for her to continue. When she did not, I prompted her. "Where have you been?"

"All over." Her voice took on a false tone of lightness when she said it.

"Really, like where?"

She seemed hard-pressed to answer. Finally she said, "All over, really. Greece. North Africa. Other places. That was a long time ago."

"Where have you been most recently?"

Tentatively she bit her lower lip, worrying it in a distracted way. She was plenty nervous about something. "You may not believe it but..."

A waiter came over to take my order. I chose the hutspot met klapstuk - a meat and vegetable stew, and had a beer to go with it. After the waiter left I looked back over at the girl. She was hurriedly picking up her gear and paying her bill and leaving the place.

"Do you have to go so soon?" I asked. She was a nice looking woman, somewhat younger than myself, and I would have liked to continue my conversation with her.

"I'm afraid so," she said, putting on her pack and then her floppy hat.

"Where are you going from here?" I said.

Again she gave an enigmatic answer. "I'll just be traveling around a little. Here and there, you know."

"Won't you tell me your name at least?" I said. I was getting desperate to keep her there, for some reason. There was something attractive about her. Perhaps it was her secretiveness.

She smiled patiently. "Sarah," she said.

"I'm Jim," I said.

"I'm very pleased to meet you."

"Won't you stay and have a beer with me?"

"I really must go. I'm sorry."

"Alright," I said.

"Goodbye," she said.

"Goodbye." I watched her go out. She turned left outside the door and walked past the big window. She walked quickly, as if fleeing someone. She did not look back.

Once I had eaten I went out to find a room for the night. There, I waited for morning. I woke up early and then waited in my darkened room until it was time for the ferry to come in. When it was time I ran through the rain-slick streets, it had rained during the night, down to the docks. The fog was back but already the sun was trying to break through. The ferry was standing tall in the fog like something from an Impressionist painting.

Over at the baggage claim window my backpack was waiting. The fat man behind the window saw me coming. He smiled and waved his smoking pipe in the air and then held up my pack to prove he had it. I smiled and waved back.

After I had claimed my baggage I turned around and there was Sarah. "Hello," she said.

"Hello, Sarah. I thought you were in a big hurry to go somewhere."

"I was," she said.

"What happened?"

"I decided not to go."

"Why not?" I seemed to be asking a lot of questions around Sarah.

"It didn't work out."

"I see." In fact, I could see nothing. "Where are you going now?"

"I don't know. Where are you going?"

"I was thinking of hitch-hiking down through Germany and Switzerland. Maybe I'll go into Italy. My itinerary is open."

"Could I go along with you?" She looked straight into my eyes.

"I don't know," I said.

"So... when will you know?"

"When you tell me what you're so afraid of. When you tell me what it is you're running from."

"It's that obvious, is it?"

"I'm afraid so," I said.

"It's just that I'm not sure you'll believe me when I tell you."

"You'll have to let me decide what I believe and what I don't believe."

"Alright," she said.

"Alright," I said.

"Here goes."

"I'm waiting."

"There's a man following me."

"What sort of man?"

"A bad man."

I glanced around. There were no men in the picture. "Why do you think this bad man is following you around?"

"He wants to kill me."

"Are you serious?" Somehow this scene was too strange to be real.

"Yes, I'm serious. Why would I lie about something like that?"

"Why does he want to kill you?"

She took a long pause. Then, "Because of what I represent."

I had to consider that for a moment. Then I asked, "What is it you represent?"

"I represent... heaven. Oh, you're not going to believe any of this."

"Heaven..." My brain had not engaged yet. I could make no connection between this woman and the alleged man following her and the word heaven. It didn't make any sense.

She began talking more rapidly now. "I don't know how it happened but I was following you around, trying to do my job, you know, trying to keep you safe when..."

"Wait a minute," I said.

She did not stop talking, but actually picked up the tempo. "...I don't know what happened. I got caught in a maze or something. Everything got all turned around and I found I couldn't get out. All at once, here I was on earth and, I don't know but I think I might also be mortal..."

"Wait a minute!" I demanded.

Sarah stopped talking.

"Are you trying to tell me that you're..." I hesitated to use the word.

"Yes," she said. "I'm an angel."

I threw back my head and laughed hard once. "What the hell is this?" I said. I was flabbergasted. This was more than I could comprehend. "Who sent you here? What is this all about?"

"No one sent me. I'm trying to tell you..."

"You're trying to tell me what. That I'm supposed to believe..."

"Oh," she stammered, "I knew you wouldn't believe me."

I laughed again. "You've got that right, sister."

SIX

Big tears welled up in Sarah's eyes.

I paid no attention to her tears. "This is too much," I exploded. "I don't know what the hell your game is..."

"Please," she said, "there is no game. You must believe me..."

"I must believe you..." I repeated with another short laugh. "You're joking, right?"

"You must believe me or I'm going to be killed."

"So you said before. The only trouble with that is, I'm not going to believe you now or ever. It doesn't matter what you say. This is really too much..." My mind was still reeling from the implications of all this. Was she crazy, or what?

"Please," she begged again.

"Please nothing. There's not a thing you can say or do to get me to believe that you're an angel..." I laughed even to hear myself say it. "... so forget it, alright?"

"Alright," she said quietly, lowering her eyes. Apparently she was going to take a different tack.

"Listen," I said, "I want you to tell me what this is all about. Is this some kind of scam or what?"

"You don't understand," she said in a pleading tone.

"You're absolutely right about that," I agreed. "I don't understand why you all would go to so much trouble. I'm not worth much. I'm not rich, if that's what you think. Or... have you got the wrong guy?"

"I don't know what you mean," she said. Indeed, she did seem to be quite confused.

"First this guy Allman sets me up to fall in step with old Frederich Nagel, and then he starts talking about angels. Then, while I'm still thinking about angels, you show up. Now, what am I supposed to make of that?"

"I'm sorry," she said, "but I don't know any of those people."

"Oh, no, of course you don't," I scoffed. "Either you know them or it was all just one big coincidence. Is that it? Is that what you expect me to believe?"

57

"I don't know," she said glumly.

"You don't know what I'm supposed to believe?"

"I don't know what you want me to say."

"I want you to say what is true!" I was growing more and more irritated with her.

"The truth is... I don't know what is the truth." Big tears squeezed out from under her lashes again and began to flow freely down her face.

All at once I felt sorry for her. Perhaps I was only being gullible again, but I suddenly had the feeling that she was telling the truth. It was the truth, at least, as far as she could know it. That could mean only one of two things; either she had been as completely duped by those two men as I, or she was insane. Upon further reflection, I began to suspect the latter. This only because I could see no earthly reason for a hoax such as was apparently being perpetrated by Allman and Nagel.

"You don't know what the truth is," I repeated at last. "I do believe that much."

"You do?"

I nodded. Where was this leading, I wondered.

"The only truth I do know is that someone, a man, is trying to kill me."

"Let's start with that, then," I said.

"Could we go some place to sit down?" She was drying her tears with the sleeve of her jacket.

We went to a nearby cafe and had coffee and pastries. While we were there she explained the whole situation to me. "This man began to follow me in New York. I don't know why. He was attracted to me, I guess. Anyway, he accosted me several times while I was in New York City and it seemed he was purposely putting himself in my way.

"Then, when I left on the plane, there he was. He followed me to London, and then here to Holland. He caught me out of my hotel last night and when I wouldn't go up to his room with him, he attacked me."

"Did he have a weapon?"

"No. He tried to strangle me." She showed me some vague marks on her neck. "He is very strong. He is like a weapon himself."

"I'm not weak myself."

"I know it," she said. "That's why I came up to you. I'd like to travel along with you. At least that way I'd be safe."

"All that makes sense," I said. "So why did you think you needed to throw in all that business about being an angel?"

"You think I'm crazy, don't you?" She lowered her head and sipped her coffee. Then she took a tiny bite of her pastry.

"I did," I said. "Now I don't know what to think."

She looked up into my eyes. "I'm not crazy, am I?"

"You might be," I said seriously. "What do you remember, from before, I mean."

"From before when?"

"Before New York. From before when this man started following you."

"It is crazy, isn't it?"

"Is it?"

"What I told you is what I remember. I've been with you since the beginning. Forever, I guess you might say. I'm the one who has been protecting you."

"Protecting me from what?" A peevish note had come into my voice.

"I know you don't believe me, and that's what scares me. You see, I think I'm totally vulnerable. I don't think I have any way of protecting myself anymore, let alone you."

"And you're going to stick by this story no matter what?" I demanded.

"I can't help it. It's what I really remember. If it's crazy, then I admit I must be crazy. And if I am, I know you might not believe me about the man. But the man is real, if you'll only believe me about that..."

"Against my better judgement, I do believe you about that."

"Thank God," she said.

"If he approaches you when I'm around, it shouldn't be too hard to run him off."

"Then... you'll let me travel with you?" she asked hopefully.

"We can travel together for a while," I told her.

Such a look of relief came into her face that I was glad I'd decided to help her. If she was insane, I reasoned, at least she did not seem violent. Chances were she'd be no trouble at all. Besides, I was lonely and in need of some female companionship. Having a woman nearby wouldn't be such a bad thing for me, either.

"You won't regret having helped me," she said. "I always knew you had a generous heart."

"You always knew? Oh yes, I see. You've been around since the beginning. Do you know what I was just thinking? It may be that you have a case of amnesia and that you've only filled in your missing memory with this preposterous story of yours."

"Do you think so?"

"It's certainly possible," I soothed. Now that I had made up my mind, I'd show her how nice I could be. "It may be that this attack caused you to blot out everything from before. Traumatic shock or something like that, I think."

"That would be great," she said, "if that's what it is. I mean, that's better than being nuts, isn't it?"

"I don't know about better. Easier to treat, perhaps."

"Oh... you think I'll need treatment?"

"I'm afraid so. Sooner or later."

"Well, that might be alright once we get away from this man who has been harassing me."

"So you do admit that it is all a fabrication," I said, hoping to pin her down to at least that.

"It is possible," she said sincerely, "but even if it is, I wish it was all true."

"Oh sure you do. That about being an angel? We all wish we were something more than we are. That's why I came on this trip in the first place, come to think of it."

"I want that to be my past because without it," she said, "I have no past."

"But what kind of past is it you have now?" It was a rhetorical question, but she answered anyway.

"My past is filled with ghosts."

"Have you ever considered that some people might prefer to go around without a personal history at all. Sometimes our past only weighs us down."

"But without a past, I don't know who I am," she objected.

"Then stick to your past of an angel for now," I said. "It's better than nothing, and it won't bother me."

"Do you mean it?" she said enthusiastically, as if I had just given her a special gift.

"You can be anything you want. We can make a game of it."

I do not now know why I was so willing to go along with all this. After all, this lady was either crazy or she was being pursued by a maniac of some kind, or both. Either way alarm bells should have been going off in my head. Instead, however, I was taking the whole thing as just another part of the adventure package. A strange adventure, to be sure, but an adventure none-the-less.

It wasn't only loneliness that was holding me near the girl in spite of all her madness. No, I had experienced loneliness before. Perhaps you would have had to see her there, sipping her coffee, to understand. She was lovely, of course. Her hair was auburn and her skin was milky white, for lack of any better description. But it was her eyes that were most captivating. They were the eyes of autumn, coffee brown in color with flecks of green and chocolate thrown in, like leaves scattering before the wind. I could not keep from looking into them.

She caught my gaze unexpectedly and held it to herself. At first she smiled nervously but then she dropped even that pretense and we just looked at each other. What passed between us was like a promise that is made, never to be broken. It was a vow, in short, yet neither of us really knew what it was we were committing to.

Then we looked away from each other. "We'd better get going," I said. What am I letting myself in for? I was wondering. All my life I have been exposed to madness and here I was confronted with it again, in this young lady this time.

"Yes," she said, "we'd better go."

"I was thinking of hitch-hiking," I said.

"They call it auto-stopping here."

"You don't mind traveling that way?"

"I've done it before," she assured me.

"You have all the gear you need, then?"

"I've come this far," she said. "I'll be just fine, no matter what. Just don't worry about me at all. It's supposed to be the other way around, you know."

"What do you mean?" I asked vaguely, still not picking up on her insistence to stick to her particular view of the past.

"I've looked after your welfare for so long..."

"You mean the angel thing again."

She nodded solemnly. "Correct."

"I'm sure I can take care of myself," I said.

She took a quick breath and shifted her eyes upward. Then, seeing my concern she said, "I'm sorry. Just a little angel superstition, I guess."

"What are you being superstitious about?"

"Whenever an angel hears someone say they can take care of themselves, we always know something is going to happen to that person. It makes extra work for us."

"I see," I said, still trying to play along.

"The trouble is," she said seriously, "you no longer have an angel. That is, I'm still your angel, but I don't think I'm an angel any more."

"Come on," I said. "You're giving me a headache with all this talk." I don't know why I can't ever have a simple, normal life. I'm always running into craziness at every turn and it was becoming a little tiresome.

Sarah followed me outside. I took out my Baedeker map and began to study it. She came up close to my ear, then, and whispered, "You've got to promise me one thing, okay?"

"Yes, well, what is it?" My annoyance must have come through loud and clear.

"Please promise me you'll take extra special care from now on."

"Oh sure, I'll be extra careful. What's the matter, don't you think they'll assign me another angel?"

"I know you're laughing at me," she pouted. "Go ahead and laugh. Do whatever you want. Only, please, just be extra special cautious in everything you do."

"I promise," I said, to be done with this topic. Still, I'm sure she could see the mockery behind my words. She was not good with mockery. She just continued on as if my words had been sincere.

"Thankyou," she said with a deep sigh. "You don't know how relieved I am to hear you say that."

It seemed to me as if we had been doing an awful lot of talking and all I'd gotten so far was a load of nonsense. I was ready to be going.

We headed out of town with our backpacks on our backs and we kept the chit-chat to a minimum. At once we began hitching toward the German border. We caught a few short rides right away. In the afternoon it began to rain again and we pulled on ponchos.

"We must be close to the border by now," Sarah said at one point.

"That's some way away yet," I corrected. "Look over there." I pointed.

"A windmill," she said in delight.

"I want to get a picture of it. We can cut across the fields - I don't think anyone will mind."

The windmill was some way distant but we had no trouble getting to it and taking some photos. Then, just as we were making ready to leave, a little green Volkswagen pulled up and two German Polizei stepped out.

"I think we're in Germany," Sarah said. "I knew we were close."

The officers spoke little English but managed to point out the direction to the nearest regular border crossing. "Dis ist not good, cutting across," one said. They proved their displeasure by having us both unpack all of our things so they could be inspected meticulously. The rain had let up a little, so we didn't get too wet.

"Who would have guessed they'd have windmills in Germany," I said in a disgusted tone.

"This would never have happened," Sarah said, "if I'd been watching over things."

"Don't start," I said. "I'm wet. I'm tired. I don't want to hear any more of this angel business for one day."

She pouted a little. "I get wet and tired too, you know."

When we had officially crossed into Germany, we hitched down to Kevelaer where we stayed in a small hostel, in separate rooms, of course. That night, before I succumbed to sleep, I caught myself chuckling about this angel I had traveling with me. I mean, it was ridiculous, right? Where would an angel get the money to pay for her room.

Anyway, we hadn't seen hide nor hair of this bad man who was supposedly following her around. That was good. What that meant was that soon I could make the decision whether to keep traveling with her, or to head out on my own again. At some point I would have to make up my mind. Was I only here to protect her, or was I really attracted to her as well. And, if I was so attracted to her, was she worth all of the trouble she was going to cause me. It would be a tough decision.

In the morning I asked Sarah to tell me something more about the man who had been following her. What did he look like. How had she first met him, and so on.

"He's big," she said. "Taller than you and..." she held her hands out from her shoulders, "... you know, bigger."

"I get the picture," I said.

"He's like a giant nutcracker, like those in the Nutcracker Ballet, with a huge square mouth that could crush your head between its teeth."

"Don't get carried away," I cautioned.

"You haven't heard the half of it. He's a psychopath."

I had visions of her going off the deep end at any time, and me having to deal with getting her into a mental institution of some kind. "Just give me the facts, if you don't mind."

"He has very short hair and swarthy, healthy skin. His hands are big. Everything on him is big."

"Alright, he's a big guy. He's a worthy opponent, if I should ever happen to run into him. How is it you came to meet him in the first place?"

"He just started following me around. I noticed him several days before he actually caught up with me. I was in a restaurant and he just came over and took a chair at my table. He started right in talking like he had known me all his life."

"And had you... known him before?"

"No, of course not. I don't know people like him. He's a born killer, I can tell."

"How can you tell?"

"It's his eyes. They're flat and cold. They're the coldest eyes you've ever seen. And he is big enough to throw an ox."

"That doesn't make him a killer," I said.

"He introduced himself to me as Morton Toombs," she said patiently. "At first I didn't make the connection."

"Wait a minute here. You didn't make what connection?"

"He's an angel from hell, you see. A fallen angel, you might say. An anti-angel, we call them."

It took a long moment for this to register. Then I said, "Oh brother, here we go again."

"Will you let me finish?" she said sternly.

"Sure. By all means. Go right ahead. I'm just dying to hear it."

"Morton Toombs is an anti-angel who has come to earth to hunt me down and kill me. He may even have been the one responsible for my being here in the first place."

"Let's go over that part again, shall we? The part about how you came to be here at all."

"Well, I was following you around, just as I have been all along - it's my job, as I told you - when I got lost. I don't really know how it happened. Suddenly I seemed to be caught in this maze and I couldn't find my way out of it. You went on without me. I was so afraid."

"Where was I when this happened?"

"You were in New York City. We were all in New York. You went down into this area of the city where I knew something terrible was going to happen to you. You were with someone who was stealing something. I kept the clerk from seeing you. I don't know. I guess that's the last I remember about that."

I was shocked, as you might well imagine. How could she have known about any of that? "What are you," I sputtered, "some kind of psychic or something?"

"I don't know what I am," she said. "That's the whole trouble, isn't it. I really believe I am your guardian angel and if that's crazy, then I guess I'm crazy. It's all I know. I have to stick with that."

"Easy," I cautioned. "Don't get yourself all worked up."

"I wish I could be as calm as you," she said.

"A level head is always better."

"It's not so easy to keep a level head when you've got someone like Morton Toombs on your tail. They're indestructible, you know."

"Anti-angels?" I smiled.

"They're practically immortal. The only way to kill one is to completely submerge him in water. It's their fire and brimstone makeup, I guess."

"So if I ever run across this guy, I should just dunk him under, is that it?" I mocked.

"That might not be as easy as it sounds," she advised.

"Well in any case, I haven't seen him around, have you?"

"Not since we left Holland. But he's following me, I know it. They never stop. They just keep coming. He'll find me sooner or later, you can bet on that."

"How terrible for you," I said. I was beginning not to believe, even, in this unseen psychopath. It was quite possible, after all, that she was making the whole thing up.

"I've gone too far again, haven't I?"

"Tell me one more thing. How is it you managed to elude this anti-angel creature once he had hold of you? I mean, why didn't he simply strangle you to death when he had the chance?"

"I threw a glass of water in his face. It burned him terribly."

"So this is something like the wicked witch from the Wizard of Oz, is it?"

"Exactly! They abhor water. Still, it doesn't stop them any unless they're completely submerged. That vaporizes them for good."

"Have you stopped to consider," I said thoughtfully, "what I must think about all this. I mean, I'm only human, you know. Didn't you think I'd have a little trouble believing your story."

"Oh I did consider that," she said. "I almost didn't tell you at first. But then, I didn't really see any way around telling you. You're involved in this whether you want to be or not, and I decided I'd better warn you."

"I see. So now that I do know, what am I going to do about it. Am I going to stick by you or am I going to leave you behind somewhere?"

"That's up to you," she said fearfully, "but I think we'd have a much better chance if we'd stay together."

"Why do you say that?"

"Because we've always been together, and with any luck, we always will be."

SEVEN

We had some little trouble making our way through Germany. The country was orderly and wooded, just as I recalled from my army days, but rides were few and far between. We walked and walked. The pack straps cut into our shoulders. The weather grew cold. At this point in our travels together I really did not know what to make of the stories Sarah had told me. I wanted us to go along as if nothing out of the ordinary was happening, but my attraction to her continued to grow, it seemed, in direct proportion to the multitude of reasons that warned me away. Was my emotional attachment, then, overwhelming my better judgement?

One thing was certain through all this; I should never have encouraged her in the angel business. Still, it was something I just could not let go of. For one thing, I was curious as to how she'd started on that particular story, and for another I wondered why she stuck with it, when it was obviously madness.

I wanted to know all about it, of course, but I didn't know quite where to begin. What questions does one ask a woman who believes she is an angel stripped of her wings? There seems to be no protocol for it. I would simply have to wade in and see where it led me.

"So tell me," I said in an offhand manner, to get the ball rolling in that direction again, "what kind of angel are you?"

"What kind?" she said, cocking her head slightly.

We had come perhaps a hundred miles into Germany now, having caught several short rides, and we were resting in a shaded area beside the road.

"Yes," I continued, "what kind. What kind as in Seraphim, Cherubim... Archangel." This last I added as an afterthought.

"Oh no, there have only been two Archangels in all eternity. There is only one now."

"Why only one?"

"Michael is the only one. The other was Lucifer, before the fall. I'm only a lowly guardian, I'm afraid. There are so many of us, we're quite commonplace."

"He will give his angels charge of you," I read from the little RSV Bible I carried in my pack, "to guard you in all your ways. On their hands they will bear you up, lest you dash your foot against a stone. Psalm 91:11."

Sarah turned to look at me. She had just been drinking water from a plastic bottle. A large Mercedes truck passed on the road. She smiled a large, real smile. "You know your Bible, don't you?"

"I study everything," I nodded, trying not to sound immodest about it.

"What's the sudden interest in the angelic mysteries?" she asked. Then, intuitively, "Ah, you want to see if I really know my stuff, is that it. Well, mister, fire away. I'll answer any question you have."

"And do you... know your stuff?" I asked her.

She continued to look seriously into my eyes. "I don't think your questions are going to make you believe me, but if they make you feel better, I'll do my best to answer them."

She was right, of course. There was nothing she could say that would convince me she was an angel, so why had I even begun this line of questioning? Probably, I now reasoned, only to show off my own broad knowledge.

I am a self-educated man, you see. During my army days I took college courses, but I was never serious about getting a degree. In the classes I liked, I did very well, while in the classes I didn't care for, I did terrible. I did well in English and History and Art, but not so well in Math and Science. These so-called hard subjects bored me to tears. Anyway, I sometimes felt inferior when it came to my knowledge and how I had come to acquire it. I was always quick to show off what I did know, to toot my own horn, so to speak. This, I think, often made me seem obnoxious.

"What is it you want to ask me?" Sarah prompted.

"I'm thinking, I'm thinking," I said, stalling for time. I flipped through the pages of my Bible. I should have been trying to put a stop to this nonsense once and for all, but here I was instead, making a damned fool of myself, asking questions that would have been better left unasked. After all, what would happen if I found her out in a mistake? Would she then lose all grasp of reality, just as my boss had done? It was certainly possible.

"What is it?" she asked. "Are you afraid you'll harm me in some way with your questions?"

"Yes," I said, nodding. "I'm afraid I'll push you right over the edge."

"Don't be afraid," she said. "Either I'm already over the edge, or I'm exactly what I say I am. To tell you the truth, I'm not quite sure myself. I'd like to know if I can answer your questions."

"I don't know that your answers will prove anything," I objected. "Just as you said, I may not believe you in any case. A good Bible student could answer all of the questions I might know to ask."

"But it would be a step in the right direction, wouldn't it?" she said. "At least then, if I couldn't answer your questions, you'd know for sure I wasn't an angel at all."

"That's true, isn't it?" I said, surprised by her reasoning.

"Please, ask away."

"Alright," I said, "let's give it a try."

"Are they hard, the questions you've been concocting in your head?"

"Some are," I said apologetically.

She seemed almost relieved to hear this. She was excited to begin, as if she really did mean to find out at last if she was what she said she was.

"I'm ready," she said expectantly.

"Why are there angels?" I asked simply.

"Angels are used to help God work His plan on earth. It was an angel that shut the mouths of the lions against Daniel and who saved Shadrach, Meshach and Abednego from the flames of the furnace. We have the ability to change form and to run back and forth between heaven and earth. We don't have earthly bodies, though. That is... we don't normally."

"Are angels strong?" I asked.

"Like the arm of God," she said. "An angel destroyed the first born of Egypt and it was a single angel that killed a hundred and eighty-five thousand men at the Assyrian encampment in II Kings 19."

"If you are so strong, then what do you have to fear?" I slipped in.

"I'm not strong now," she said. Again her eyes became watery. "It's such a wonderful state to be in... I don't know what I'm doing here. I'm human, I guess."

"It would seem so," I said flatly.

"I don't fear death, though. I've seen enough of it to know what happens. An angel comes for us, you know. There is nothing to fear. We just go home."

"If you don't fear death," I said, "then what do you have to fear from the likes of this maniac, this Morton Toombs?"

"That's different," she replied quickly. "That's not death. If he catches me, he'll take me along to hell with him. That I do fear."

"So there is a hell then?"

"Not the way you think of it, probably."

"Tell me about it."

"When we die, we can go to heaven, which is like the spirit going home again. You'll be more alive than you have ever been in life on earth. That is the real life."

"And hell?"

"It's torment. There, you can never have what you want. You always want more. Or, sometimes, you can have everything you want. Do you see what I mean?"

"Frankly, I don't."

"If in life, say, you had been a glutton, and your gluttony had gotten in the way of your spirit's return to its pure state. Then in hell you would be given every kind of food you loved, and you would eat and eat and you could never stop yourself. You could have everything you wanted, only after while you wouldn't want it any more. That's hell."

"So I should cut back on my eating," I said jovially, patting my slightly larger than flat stomach.

"This is not a laughing matter," she scolded. "Hell is failure. If you insist upon failure in life, you will fail in death."

"The flesh is weak," I said. "That seems like a mean thing to do to someone. If a person has a weakness in life, why should he have to pay such a price in death?"

"It's not the weakness itself," she said. "We all have weaknesses. It's what we do with it that counts. Humans are put here to grow. That's the task of living on earth. If you fail to grow, however, if you allow life to run you over, then it can stand in the way of the spirit's return. To go to hell one would have to fail over and over again at every chance he or she has been given."

"Over several lifetimes..." I interjected.

She paused. "Yes. Over several lifetimes."

"I'm sorry," I said, "but I don't remember any mention of reincarnation in the Bible."

"No," she said glumly. "You won't find it mentioned there."

"Why not?"

"Life is cyclical," she said. "Everything on earth is born and grows and decays and dies. And then it is reborn. That is how life regenerates itself. What, then, makes you think the soul is any different?"

"That doesn't answer my question," I pointed out.

"When the Bible was written, the idea of reincarnation was such an accepted one, no one thought to write it down."

"That sounds unlikely," I objected. "They seemed to have written everything else down."

"I don't have good arguments for things," she said. "I only know what's true and what's not."

"Is that supposed to be enough for me?"

At that moment a bus went by on the road. Sarah glanced up at it and then gasped. "It's him," she said in a terrified whisper.

"Who?"

"Morton Toombs."

"Where?"

"He was on that bus."

I looked up the road after the rapidly departing bus. All I could see was the rear of the thing. "Are you sure?"

"I saw his face in the window."

"What was he doing?"

"Just looking at us. Looking and laughing."

"How can you be sure it was him?"

"I'm sure," she said. "I'll never forget that face as long as I live."

"But it was moving so fast..."

"It was him."

She sounded so sure of herself, it made me stop and think. Then, "What do you think he was doing?"

"He's found us," she said. "He's gone on ahead somewhere to wait for us."

"You think we should go back?"

"I don't know what we should do," she said. I could hear the desperation in her voice.

"Don't go getting yourself all upset," I said. "He's probably not going to come around as long as you're with me."

"You don't know what he's capable of. He'll take us both if we're not careful."

"To hell?" I prompted. I thought by saying it she would hear how ridiculous it sounded.

"That's right."

"I've never been there," I said. "Have you."

She closed her eyes and crossed the fingers of both hands, index and middle together. "Don't ever say that," she said, "even in jest."

"I wasn't jesting," I said. "Have you ever been there?"

"Of course not."

"But Toombs has been."

"He comes from there, I already told you."

"What do you think it's like?"

"It's a place of misery. We shouldn't even be discussing it."

"Well, you see, that's the thing about being human, you don't have to worry too much about the rules."

"Maybe you should worry about them a little more."

"We humans don't mind taking a chance if it means we might learn something. We're pretty curious, don't you know. Why do you think Adam and Eve ate that apple. Look at Solomon."

"Solomon?" she questioned.

"Solomon and his magic ring."

"I don't know about his ring."

"Aha," I said. "He had a ring that the people of his time believed could change the course of events. They believed it was given him by God."

"Solomon was in jeopardy of losing everything," she said, "with all his curiosity."

"My point exactly," I said triumphantly. "If Solomon was the wisest of the wise, it was only because he continued learning long after others had counted themselves learned."

"I don't know much about being human, I guess," she said wistfully. "I miss being me."

"If you aren't you, who are you?" I asked.

"I'm so confused," she admitted now, slumping down into herself. "I think I'm only part of who I was. I think I had to give something up to get into a human body."

"That may be true for all of us," I reflected. "In any case, we'd better get a move on. We're not getting very far at this rate."

"Do you think we should, under the circumstances?"

"What... oh, you mean with old Mister Toombs up ahead, do you. Well, let's just continue on our course as if nothing is going on, and then we'll see what happens."

"You may not want to see," she said fearfully. "Don't forget, there's no one around to protect us now."

"What about God?" I said.

"There's always God," she replied. "But we have to look out for ourselves too."

We caught several rides that afternoon which took us as far as Mayen, which was off our route. There, the city seemed never to end. There were cement factories on both sides of the road. It grew dark and we still had not found an inn. We walked and walked. Both of us became exhausted. We stumbled along.

The bells of a church struck eleven. On the right was a field of wheat. "What do you think," I asked. "Should we stay here tonight?"

"Right now, I'm ready for anything."

We laid our sleeping bags out in the field and settled in for some sleep. Far off, the bells struck eleven thirty.

While I lay there listening to the unfamiliar sounds of that night-blanketed field, I began to think about the possibilities of all that had been told me. Mine is not a mind for mysteries. (Have I made that clear enough?) I like practical things in life and good old American realism in art and literature. The modern times are confusing enough without surrounding one's self with even more perplexing ideas. There is, and I thought should be, a move afoot to return to the solid things of the past in religion, in values, and in arts and crafts, (thus the craving for antiques).

In life, as in the writing of this book, I am attempting to capture all of the essential details. I fear uncertainty. Ever since I first began to understand how insanity stalks the world, I have shunned those things that cannot be seen or touched. That which is not tangible, which is not concrete, is unreal, and thus an ingredient of madness. I abhor it, and want nothing at all to do with it.

So you can see how this talk of the angelic mysteries was affecting me. If it had not been for my attraction to this woman, and at the time I must admit it was an almost purely physical attraction, I would have slipped away from her as I had done old Herr Nagel. All along I had been trying to hold the world absolutely still while I lived my life under my own control, but now Sarah was threatening this in two ways. In the first place she was unsettling me with her great beauty - her alluring beauty of a woman, and in the second place she was presenting herself to me as some kind of trapped angel - something I certainly could not accept as true. She was a dilemma in the flesh.

She murmured something in her sleep and then rolled over. Her face was inches from my own. Though it was dark here, I could see the whole outline of her face glowing in my memories. I had no doubt that I should pick up now and clear out. To stay was to face an immediate future of such uncertainty that I knew I would be totally unprepared to deal with it. This was a trap, I was sure, and to stay longer would be a grave mistake. Still, I seemed unable to pull myself away. I seemed unable to withdraw from this web that bound us together in anticipation of the morrow.

I wanted to kiss her lips. Their presence was so tempting. My heart throbbed within me. If I were to kiss them now, would she awaken?

Then, with great determination, I rolled over and faced the other direction, turning my back to her. What was happening to me?

Eventually my mind quieted. I really was sleepy. My eyes closed.

The next thing I remember, the bells were striking five. We got up and again headed out onto the road. Neither of us were doing much talking then. My eyes were still puffy from sleep and hers looked the same.

"We're never going to get to Frankfurt," she lamented, "if we don't get a ride pretty soon."

"Maybe we should catch a bus or a train or something."

"It's against my principles," she joked, "but if we don't get a ride soon, I'll agree."

Huge lumber trucks growled past us. None of them stopped. The day grew hot and wearisome.

In Koblenz we took the train to Frankfurt, following the Rhine down through the steep walls of the hills. It was late afternoon when we finally arrived. We took rooms with high ceilings in a charming hotel five minutes walk to the south of the Hauptbahnhof off Dusseldorfstrasse. Straight away Sarah went to her room to take a nap.

"I'm exhausted," she said.

"Once I get a bath, I'm going out exploring," I told her. "I might not be back until later."

"That's fine," she said with a shrug. "I'd go with you only I'm just too tired."

"Get some rest," I said.

Once I had taken my bath in a tub with claw legs, I headed out onto the street. I followed Kaiserstrasse along toward the center of the city and then ran into the Fressgasse which is lined with quaint cafes and restaurants. Along there, a curious thing happened. A man called to me in English.

"Come on over," he hailed, waving his arm. He was sitting at a small cafe table that was situated under an awning, and he was drinking a beer. He dwarfed everything around him; the table, chair, and the German people sitting near him.

I hesitated. He looked oddly familiar. There was something about his big square face and straight mouth that I remembered from somewhere. Trouble is, I've lived long enough now that everyone looks vaguely familiar and I could not place him. Had I met him in army days? Was he an old construction buddy of mine from another time? I could not recall.

"Would you care for a beer?" he called heartily. He was definitely an American.

Still, I hesitated longer. I felt dumb standing uncertainly there on the sidewalk. Who was he? I racked my brain.

"What's the matter," he said, "don't you drink beer?"

"I drink beer," I said defensively.

"Come drink one then." He had won his hand, and he knew it. What else was I going to do at this point?

I went over to his table. "Do I know you?" I asked bluntly.

"Sit down. Take a load off." He directed me to a chair with his big forefinger.

I sat in the chair he had pointed out. "I know you from somewhere..." I said thoughtfully.

He ordered a beer, using rudimentary German. "Ein bier, bitte." Then he turned back to me. "You may not know me," he said enigmatically.

The beer came in a big mug and he pointed the waiter over to me. The man set the glass in front of me and withdrew at once. The big American made him nervous, apparently.

"When you called me over," I continued, "I thought sure I knew you from somewhere."

"Perhaps someone described me to you," he said with a sly laugh.

That information only deepened the mystery of the moment. Who would have described him to me? 'Oh!' A sudden light of realization popped on in my brain. Panic squeezed a pit in my stomach. Could this be the man Sarah had talked about? I looked closer. Indeed, he had the face and features of a giant nutcracker, just as she had said. "Are you..."

"She has told you about me," he said triumphantly.

I eased my glass mug up to my lips, buying time. In fact, I did not know what to make of this seemingly accidental meeting. As I set the mug down I said, "If you are Mister Toombs, then... yes, she has told me about you."

"Morton Toombs is my name," he said, giving me another of his grins.

"What is it you want from me?" I asked.

"I'm trying to catch up with Sarah," he said directly.

"Why are you following her?"

He seemed surprised by the question. "Why... I'm her husband. I want to take her home."

Taken aback by this new information, I did not quite know what to say next. "She... she never mentioned that she was married." I was confused and disheartened at the same time. Why had she kept this from me? Was it even true? Perhaps she didn't know the truth herself.

"We've had our differences, Sarah and I. She's not well, you know. You may even have guessed that yourself."

"Well, yes. I did have some question about the things she told me. But I never considered that you might actually be..." (I hesitated to even say it,) "... her husband."

"She needs treatment," he said. "I've come to take her home and get her taken care of."

"Where will you take her?" I asked. "Where is home?"

"Where did she tell you home was?"

"She didn't say."

"Then why do you ask me?" He suspected a trick. The grin was swiped off his face.

"I was making conversation. I wondered what kind of home you had, that's all."

"There's no more time for conversation," he snapped through his big teeth. "I demand to know where she is."

"Don't be in such a hurry," I said, reeling back a little in my chair. The force of his demand had taken me off my guard.

"You don't want to get in my way," he said fiercely. "I'll crush you. Now tell me where she is at once and we will go!"

"Not so fast," I cautioned. "After some of the things she told me, I'm not going to be quick to hand her over." My jaw was set firmly now. "I hope you understand that it's for her protection."

"I don't understand anything. If you believe all that nonsense about angels and about me attacking her..." He realized his mistake even as he made it.

"How did you know about that?" I asked evenly.

He stopped talking and his eyebrows pulled down narrowly from his forehead. His mistake was plain enough, even to himself, so he tried a different tactic. "I am a hater of many things," he said. "Desist in your harboring of this woman lest you become one of them."

"You don't scare me," I said, looking him straight in the eye.

He laughed caustically. "Desist, cousin. I'll not warn you again."

I stood up. He stayed where he was. By the look of him, there was much to fear.

EIGHT

I hurried back to the hotel, glancing over my shoulder at every turn to be sure Toombs was not following. When I arrived I pounded on Sarah's door and called her name. After a minute she opened it cautiously, looking as if I had awakened her from a deep sleep. "Yes," she said, "what is it?"

"It's him," I said, "Toombs. He's here in Frankfurt. I just saw him downtown."

Her eyes widened, her sleep abandoned now. "Is he coming? Yes, of course he is. He'll never let us go."

"He didn't follow me," I said defensively.

"That doesn't matter. He can find me wherever I go. Oh, I don't know why I got you involved in this. It's all over for me. He'll only take you with me, if you get in his way."

"He won't get to you," I vowed, "as long as you're with me."

"You don't even know what you're talking about!" she said, shaking her head vigorously. "You don't have any idea about what you're up against."

"He's big," I admitted, "but I've been around a little. Besides, I think I'm going to call the police - the polizei, and get some help."

"That'll never work," she said. "They couldn't do anything against him. They wouldn't help us anyway..."

"Sure they would," I interrupted.

"What would we tell them?"

"We'd tell them the truth."

"They wouldn't believe that..."

"Not that crap about the angels and what-not," I said shortly. "I mean the real truth. We have to tell them that we have a psychopath on our trail. That is the truth, isn't it?"

"Yes, of course. Why, what did he tell you?"

"He said he was your husband."

"Oh my God!" Sudden tears welled up in her eyes. "You didn't believe him, did you?"

"Is it true?"

78

"That's what he'd like," she whispered. "Then I'd be his evil bride for all eternity."

"Let's knock off that eternity stuff and worry about the present moment, alright?"

She nodded solemnly. "I'm sorry," she said, "but please, don't call the police. Let's just get out of here."

"I'd like to know why you're so dead set against the police."

"By the time they could get here, we'd both be dead. Believe me, he'll stop at nothing. If they protected us for the time being, he'd just catch us later. The sooner we get out of here, the better." Her voice had taken on such a desperate tone, I simply could not ignore what she was saying.

"I understand you're afraid," I soothed, "but don't you think we'd be better off to get some protection? What can we do to save ourselves from the likes of him without weapons?"

"Weapons won't mean a thing. He'll keep coming no matter what anyone does. The only thing we can do is run and hope we get away from him somehow."

"I don't know why I'm going along with all this," I said, "but I guess we can go. We can get the next train out to anywhere."

She was so happy at the news that she threw her arms around my neck and kissed me full on the lips. I kissed back. We could not resist each other.

After a long moment she pulled away and stepped back, breathlessly. "I'm sorry," she said.

"I didn't mind," I said.

She smiled and then put her lips together as if savoring my taste on them. Then she turned and quickly began to throw her things into her backpack. "I'll be just a minute," she said.

"I'll go over and pack my things too," I said. "Come over as soon as you're done."

Once we had finished our packing we rushed up the strasse to the cavernous Hauptbahnhof. The first train out was heading for Bern, Switzerland. It left the station in twenty minutes. We bought tickets and then a couple of German chocolate bars with hazelnuts which we munched quickly. We boarded the train and waited impatiently for it to be off, watching along the platform all the time for Toombs. He never showed.

When the train bumped once and then began to move up the track, we both slumped back into our seats and relaxed. "I didn't see him, did you?" she asked.

"No. He didn't get on this train that I could see."

"He wouldn't have known what train we were getting on in any case," Sarah said. "But I'm always nervous about him."

"I noticed that."

She laughed freely for a moment and then her face turned serious. "I really want to thank you for all your help."

"You don't need to thank me," I objected. "It's turning out to be quite an adventure."

"I hope it doesn't become more adventure than you bargained for," she warned.

"Let me worry about that."

"Once a fallen angel gets his teeth into something, he never lets go. He'll follow us until he catches us. And then..."

"Don't talk about that," I said. I was trying to be kind. Still, this constant talk about angels was wearing on me. It reminded me time and time again of the need to get her some form of psychological help. How and where this could be done, I hadn't a clue.

Sunlight flashed into the windows. The clacking sound of the rails beneath us became constant and uniform. We were on our way to Switzerland. The day was disappearing in the west. Sarah settled back further in her seat and closed her eyes. I watched her for a time.

Surprisingly, no one had joined us in our compartment. The platform had been full of people. Not that I was complaining, mind you. It was strange, however.

Then, after the train had departed, a portly German man entered our compartment tentatively, smiled, and, after placing the lone suitcase in the rack overhead, sat himself down.

"Guten tag," I said.

The man nodded openly and said, "Guten tag." Then, at once, he launched into a long story of some kind, completely in German, and I was lost in the dust. My German does not extend far beyond getting directions and ordering a meal. This did not deter our friend, however. He went on and on, apparently expanding his story as he continued. I tried to stop him once and explain my plight but he seemed not to care a wit.

At last he finished his story and laughed and laughed. We laughed along with him, though without so much vigor since we had no idea what there was to laugh about. He settled back then, and closed his eyes.

Sarah and I glanced at each other, and could barely conceal the mirth in our faces.

Outside, the day had remained pleasant and now the sun was leaning more and more toward the west. Along the way there were the lights and warning bells at the crossings as we went through them, and the wheels of the train kept up their regular clatter. A man in corduroy pants and rubber boots was fishing along a river. Beyond him the hillside was terraced with grape vines. There was a town of timber frame houses, a square with a tall bronze statue, and the spires of a cathedral on the other side. A factory was billowing white smoke. Then we crossed a steel bridge over the river and began making our way up into the hills.

After ten minutes our German friend stood up abruptly and, rummaging through his suitcase, he produced a brown paper wrapping which held, he revealed to us in triumph, a long sausage and crusts of rye bread. Through his motions he led us to understand that we were to share this feast with him.

"You know, I didn't realize how hungry I was," Sarah told me.

"Well, maybe we should go to the dining car rather than eat up all this man's food."

"That's a good idea. I'm famished. That little bit of sausage won't be enough for me."

With motions and with my minuscule German, I managed to convey our intentions to him. As soon as he figured out what I meant he set to eating his feast, and did not look up at us again. We made our way up the aisle, which swayed up and down like the deck of a ship, in the direction of the dining car.

The tables were mostly occupied, though we did find one on the far side, a small one big enough for just the two of us. We ordered trout and rice and carrots, and split a bottle of Mosel-Saar-Ruhr wine. The waiters rushed up and down between the tables with trays balanced in their hands. The place was quite busy.

When we finished we could see the rails gleaming along the curve in the tracks ahead in the last of the sunlight. It grew dark abruptly while we drank the rest of our wine. The last thing I could make out clearly was an onion-tower church off by itself beside a small lake.

"Isn't it wonderful?" Sarah said, turning to look at me.

"It would be wonderful if we didn't have that freak chasing us all over the place."

"I'm so glad you decided to come with me. I could never have made it through all this without you."

"That's nice to know. Do you think we've managed to elude him?"

"No," she said. "We've escaped for the time being, but there's no telling when he'll find us again. He has a great sense for that kind of thing."

"Well in any case, we can relax for the time being."

We went back up to our compartment. The light was blazing through the window, out into the passageway. Our German friend looked up and waved as we opened the door. He had finished his sausage and bread, apparently, and a half full bottle of beer sat in the seat beside him. It was the kind of bottle with the ceramic stopper strapped down with wire. We went in and settled back into our seats across from him.

Sarah yawned. "Oh. That wine made me sleepy."

"You never did get much of a nap. Why don't you lay back and sleep. We won't be in Bern until midnight or there abouts."

"That does sound pretty good."

I reached over to lower the blind at the window. Before I did, however, I looked askance at the German man across from us. "Sehr gut?" I asked.

"Ja. Das ist good. Ein Schlafen. Schlafen-gehen." He made a pillowing motion with his hands. Then he turned away, as to mind his own business, and picked up his bottle of beer. Before many seconds, while he drank, the whole compartment had filled up with the smell of beer.

Sarah leaned back into the corner created by the seat and the outside wall of the train, and was asleep almost at once. I closed my eyes and dozed sitting up for several minutes. Then, as I fell asleep, I must have leaned over and rested my head on her shoulder. We were awakened some time later by an officer coming in to check passports as we were crossing into Switzerland.

I looked sheepishly at Sarah. "I'm sorry I was sleeping on you. I must have been pretty tired too."

"I don't mind," she said through the haze of her interrupted sleep. "You can lean on me."

Minutes later we were asleep again.

With the arrival of Morton Toombs on the scene, there in Frankfurt, my situation had drastically changed. Though I could not seriously entertain the idea that he might be a fallen angel as Sarah suggested, he was indeed a threat to us. We were no longer enjoying a simple vacation, visiting castles and cathedrals and sampling various goodies along our route. No, my journey had taken a sudden bizarre turning, and it had all begun with the meeting of this woman. What kind of person was she, really? Where had she come from. How had she spent her childhood. These were some of the questions I had begun to ask myself. There were so many things I did not know about her, in fact, that I was beginning to be bothered by my lack of discrimination in choosing a traveling companion. I mean, my relationship to her had changed, had it not. She was no longer only a chance acquaintance I had decided to take under my wing. We had now entered upon a strange and tricky path that could, in the end, lead us to our deaths. Did I trust her enough to put my very life in her hands.

And this Morton Toombs fellow; what was I to make of him. I certainly did not believe he was Sarah's husband, his warnings had made that clear enough. But who was he? Where had he come from and why was he following her around. It seemed unusual to me, though I am no expert on the subject by any means, that a psychopath would choose one particular woman to track and attempt to kill. There were plenty of other women around, many of whom would fit Sarah's basic physical profile. Why did he not choose one of them?

But more than either of these mysteries, what was I to make of my own foolish actions. Was I not by nature a cautious man, so resistant to those uncertain areas of my life that might over time lead to horrible insanity. Why, then, was I treading on this unstable ground? What of my practical personality and my unshakable grip on reality? Would I now allow myself to fall for the sake of this woman. And if I did fall, where would I find the bottom?

Somewhere just outside the city of Bern we were awakened again as the door of the compartment slid open with a hiss. I could barely get my eyes open, so everything seemed to be happening in a dream.

Morton Toombs came in from the passageway. Our German friend woke up and looked at him in surprise. The big man stepped over my legs and grabbed Sarah by the hair. She came fully awake with a start. "Hey, what are you doing?" Then she saw who it was and fear came into her eyes.

Our German friend stood up at once and tried to pry the big man's hands loose from her hair. Toombs hit him in the upper chest, just below the throat, with such force that the man fell back and passed out.

I lunged up out of my seat and pushed Toombs over on top of the German. In the process his hand let loose of Sarah's hair. I took her arm and urged her along into the passageway with me. We turned to the right, toward the front of the train, and lurched up the way.

"How did he find us?" I wondered aloud.

"He'll always find us," Sarah said, looking over her shoulder.

It did not take long for Morton Toombs to recover himself. He jumped out into the passage and looked up both ways until he spotted us just leaving the car. The sudden noise between the cars was so loud as to be startling. Then we were in the next car and rushing forward.

We were not going to make it. We couldn't escape him. He was going to catch us before we made it through this car. In desperation I reached over and pulled the emergency cord that ran along above the windows. "Hang on," I said just before I did it.

I have never done this before, of course, and have only seen it done in movies, but it worked. At once the big metal wheels of the train began to squall their protest against the steel rails. The train stopped so abruptly that Toombs was jerked off his feet and thrown to the floor. I managed to stay upright, knowing what was coming, by holding onto the rim around one of the windows. Sarah held onto me.

Even before the train had stopped moving I threw open the door between the next two cars and leapt out, taking Sarah with me. We were out in the dark, suddenly, with only the lights of the distant city to guide us. With me in the lead we plowed down through the loose grading along the tracks and into a copse of trees that ran along there.

"Where are we going?" Sarah asked.

"Quiet," I said. "We're going to try to lose him. It's our only chance."

We heard Toombs cursing behind us, and scrambling down from the train and into the gravel. "You sons of bitches," he yelled, "you'll never get away from me."

A police-style whistle blew in the distance. It was doubtful they would catch him. It was doubtful anyone could catch him. He came and went as he pleased, it seemed, and did whatever he wanted.

"Come back here," he shouted in the darkness. Then we heard him crashing through the branches of the trees in the copse.

Meanwhile we exited the other side, and came onto a residential lane. We followed this down for several hundred feet, and then cut off through a narrow alley blanketed in complete darkness. Only the fact that it, too, ran downhill kept us going in the right direction.

Having eluded capture for the time being, we came down into the medieval streets of Bern. There were not many people about at this hour, it must have been eleven thirty or twelve. Three men came out of a bar with their arms thrown around each other. They were singing boisterously.

We came into the city from somewhere behind the Spitalgasse past the Bagpiper fountain, and down Marktgasse past the clock tower. Then we were on Kramgasse with its many fountains and, at its end, the Nydegg Church. From there, somehow, we managed to find our way back out onto the open road. This one led toward a town called Thun.

"We'll never get a ride at this time of night," Sarah said.

"No. We'll just have to find a place to sleep and then get an early start in the morning."

"You know what I just realized? We haven't got our backpacks. We left them on the train."

I hadn't realized it either. We'd be lost without them. "I hope you have your passport and money. I always keep mine in my pocket."

"I have them," she said. "But what about all of our gear?"

"We'll just have to buy more gear when we get to a town," I said. "I hope that's the end of our man Toombs."

"I do too," she said, "but somehow I don't think it is."

Just beyond town we found a little nook in the mountains and there, within a stand of pines, we huddled together and slept under the full moon.

NINE

One never knows for certain which way life will take him. That is the one aspect that makes life worth the living, I suppose. Will you become enmeshed in a sordid affair, perhaps, or be swept up in war or revolution? You can always count on the unexpected.

Who could have guessed, only a short time ago, that I would be in Switzerland, sleeping on the hard ground with a beautiful woman? What an unlikely event! Only a strange set of circumstances could have led me here, don't you agree?

I woke up at about three. Some time during the night I had rolled over and embraced Sarah. Where our bodies came together we were creating a fantastic heat, but on the other side; on my back, the air was freezing cold. The cold was also seeping into my bones from below - coming up through the ground, and my arm was numb where she lay her head upon it. Still, because of the wonderful warmth that was flowing between us, I did not yet want to move.

The moon was far over on the horizon now. The darkness was made all the sterner by its faltering light.

It was all happening so naturally between Sarah and I, that was the disconcerting part. In spite of her crazy notions and in spite of the big psychotic killer trailing us, I was falling for this woman. There, I had said it. Until now I had not wanted to even consider the idea. The whole situation was preposterous, really. How were we to fall in love while the world was reeling chaotically all around us? But I guess that is the strange thing about falling in love: when two people come together, the rest of the world ceases to exist.

Still, it was way too soon to be thinking of love or anything like it. I was greatly attracted to her, certainly, but what kind of future could there be with such an unstable woman? All along the way I have prided myself on my reason and my clarity of vision. It had become my life's work to avoid those pitfalls that might lead, as I have said before, to screaming insanity. I had paid a price for this, of course, but I paid it gladly. The coin I had ren-

87

dered was spontaneity, creativity, and imagination. My days had grown lukewarm, but at least it was time in which I had avoided the madhouse.

Now, gently, I eased my arm out from under her neck. Instantly pins of feeling prickled through the numbed skin. Sarah sighed once and brought her own arm up under her head as a make-shift pillow. I pulled myself up a little so that I could look at her in the soft light. From that vantage I could see her graceful shoulders and her ivory neck. Her brown hair was swept back and I could make out the outline of her left ear.

She was a classic beauty, rich and perfect and not at all like those loathsome willow-limbed creatures of modern advertising. While I looked at her, long sensations thrilled up my spine - was it the cold? But no, even I knew better than that. My desire was becoming dangerous.

I could no longer trust myself. Before my thoughts became any baser, I rolled over and faced away from her. After a long moment of separation I let my cold back settle along the length of her. Reacting to this cold, she turned in her sleep and put her arm around me, and across my chest. She muttered something I could not make out.

Her breasts were nuzzling a place just below my shoulder blades. I tried to put my mind on other things, but found I could not. I wanted to turn over and take her in my arms and I wanted to kiss her lips.

She was the incarnation of my desires. I no longer yearned for some young nymph to help me salvage part of my own lost youth. There would be no more frantic groping for me. More than anything in this world, I wanted to make no more mistakes.

One thing was certain; we would be adult about all this. There would be no headlong falling in love, by God! We were both old enough to have histories, you see. There could be no fooling us about love and desire.

Leave it to me to be tentative, even now, in my accounts as well as in the living of my life. What I wanted was to throw open the floodgates of love and never look back, but instead I continued sanely and privately. The emotions that seethed within were quelled so that, on the surface, they could be viewed without a single ripple. Here, even my flowery prose conceals volcanic thunder such as you can scarcely imagine, my dear reader, but I go on in my banal way, hoping that wit and charm and prudence will win out in the end over shear animal magnificence.

It is maddening, at times, to be trapped within this exterior of correctness and politeness. I seem to have somehow divorced one half of my self from the rest. On the outside I am a weak solution of a man. Oh, I'm sure I posses a certain poise, others have always told me so, and of course I have polished my use of language. But this is nothing more than a thin veil I use to disguise the rest.

What I really wanted was to send the world to blazes! I wanted lush warm darkness, not frosty aloofness. I wanted burlesque and magic acts and fascinating mysteries, not secret sufferings masked by formality and theater. I wanted love and poetry, not dry prose. I wanted a great giant smokestack of a life.

But time was running out for poor old Sanderson.

I had grown used to viewing life from a certain vantage. My feelings were quiet ones, or so it seemed. The image others saw of me rode along on the unnoticed, yet tormented, shipwreck of my soul. Where had I lost who I had once been? I wonder.

For that, I suppose I will have to return to the past again. To the solid midwestern order of my childhood. One does not risk one's soul there, I can tell you. As I grew up I felt big and dense and dull. Somehow I knew there was a larger world just beyond the borders of our town, but I could never quite see it from there. I had learned of it, to tell the truth, through literature. One ought not read unless one is prepared to do something about it, I now say.

In those days, I remember myself as a quiet, withdrawn boy. I would much rather spend time in my bedroom reading and writing, it was in my makeup even then, than out in the living room with the family, watching television or discussing the events of the day. My father, may he rest in peace now as he never could in this world, was convinced that my introverted ways would lead me straight into insanity. After all, it was the same mousey manner that the others of us who had gone mad displayed in their illness. His remonstrating, however, only made me feel inadequate and I withdrew even further.

I knew, in short, that he was absolutely right, but there was nothing at all I could do about it. I was the way I was, and there could be no changing that, no matter how hard he railed or how hard I tried. I remember actually taking a leaf in my hand and turning it over, so as to get the symbolism of change clearly in my head.

My father was a monstrous, hard-charging man, a Taurus who was every bit the bull he proclaimed himself to be. He had been a gravel hauling, excavating, house building, paint brush wielding maniac, and could never understand why I was not the same. He was sensitive too, don't get me wrong, but he was convinced that sensitiveness was not necessarily a trait to be proud of. He ruled our house with an iron hand, and my only means of evading him was to escape down inside myself.

At some point in my high school years, I believe it was around the time my grandmother killed herself, I decided I had better make a real attempt at change. Instead of writing, I would make building trades my career. If I wanted to write, I reasoned, I could always do that as a hobby, part time, on the side. Then, if I sold something or made the best seller list or whatever, I could turn to it full time. As you might have guessed by now, however, that never happened.

So the rift in my personality had begun. The quiet, intelligent genius was pushed down into his place, and the buoyant, extroverted builder of buildings took his place, and the two of them would never meet up again.

I could talk about that on and on for the remainder of this volume, I am quite sure, but it serves no purpose. What is past is past, as they say, and the future waits for no one.

Every time I pause long enough to try to pull the various parts of me back together, another surging, sloppy wave of life hits me, and I'm right back where I started. What's the use of even trying?

Still, I do wonder what my life might have been had I started out differently. What if I had been sired, for instance, by an exotic silk trader or a jewel thief, instead of a carpenter. What if I had been born to a belly-dancer or a princess or had been raised motherless. What if I'd had a nanny to read to me from 'A Thousand And One Nights'. What if mon petit papa had written saucy French novels.

Well, that didn't happen, did it. There is no way to escape. I am who I have become. There are many conflicting factors in even a simple life.

We must return to the matter at hand now; more's the pity. I could swim around in my past, feeling sorry for myself at every turn, for hours and hours. But every time I do, I return feeling empty and sad. There is no benefit to be had from it. Sarah is holding me comfortably now, and the moon is down and the cold is worse than before and I have the unbearable urge to urinate. Nothing can be done for it. I must get myself up and find the nearest available tree and stand behind it and fire my way into relief.

When I placed Sarah's hand down to her side and rolled away from her, she stirred in her sleep and said, "Where are you going?"

"I'll be back in a minute," I said. I wondered who she thought she was talking to. What was her past like?

Without another moment's delay, I scurried off into the forrest. My hands were much too cold to touch the old boy so I just let him go about his business. What a relief it was to be rid of that pressure!

Of course there were other pressures building in its place. I have a sexual history just like anyone else, only mine is rather a foolish one. Certainly not the one I had envisioned for myself way back when I first began fantasizing about such things. It began in my sophomore year in high school with a lesson. The lesson, at least, I have never forgotten.

At that time I was head over heels for a girl named Marsha. She was a tall, lovely peach of a thing and I thought I'd spend my whole life with her. Now that I think of it, I wonder why she didn't consider me strange, as I now think of myself back then. But apparently our personalities meshed alright. She was a quiet person herself, come to think of it, and had a shy, hesitant smile.

The trouble with Marsha was, she was above the rest of the world. That very well may have been her only asset, too. She was austere, like the princesses of yesteryear, and graced our days with her beautiful but regal presence. No other boy would have her, but I found her somehow intriguing. She, and me too by association, was just too good for the likes of them.

I had other needs too, however, besides just platonic ones. We were good together as long as I worshipped the ground she walked upon, but she was too coy for kissing or hugging or even snuggling, come to that.

During that school year my desk happened to be located next to the desk of a girl named Patricia. She was a good old red-blooded American girl who knew what was what when it came to boys and girls. Every boy in the class wanted her and most probably had had her too. So I suppose I was something of a challenge to her. And, in spite of my better judgement, I felt attracted to her. It was loathsome, I know. This was surely only a physical, animal attraction, and I had no right to it. But it was there between us, no matter what I thought of the matter.

One day I caught a glimpse of the top of her nylons. She had them strapped up with elastic, as was the fashion of the day. Her dress had hiked up to reveal their very tops and it took little imagination to speculate what was beyond what could be seen. Suddenly, as by design, she turned to look at me. Then, seeing what I was staring at, she smiled. Her smile was nothing at all like Marsha's. Hers was an openly taunting, lusty smile. "Do you like what you see?" she asked.

I turned red with embarrassment, I am quite sure. "Well," I stammered, "yes, I do."

She laughed slyly and then leaned over closer to me. "Why don't you meet me out under the bleachers after school," she whispered, "and I'll show you more."

I almost couldn't breath. This was an opportunity I simply could not pass up. Here, for the first time in my life, I was being offered something that had always been stewing in the very bottom of my haunted mind. "Alright," I finally managed to say, "I'll be there."

After school it was not Patricia, but Marsha who was waiting. I could tell she was mad from a long way off. I nearly turned and left, but there seemed no way out of the scene that was sure to take place.

"How could you?" she demanded, before I was even close. "You were coming down here to meet that girl. I don't believe it. She told me but... I just couldn't believe it."

Normally I am a pretty good liar but in this case I simply could find nothing to say in my own defense. I had, indeed, let Marsha and myself down. My dignity was gone. I was among the fallen. There was nothing to be said in my defense.

"You know," she said, still seething with anger, "I always thought you were better than those other boys, but now I see you're not. All you ever think about is... well... the bad thing."

"Marsha..." I said, hoping to regain some lost ground now that I was able to find my tongue.

"Don't talk," she said. "Don't bother to say anything. I don't ever want to have anything more to do with you. Not ever." With those words she stamped away across the football field and I was left there feeling like a total fool, which of course I was.

A short time later I went out with a girl named Dolores. She was a plump little dumpling of a girl I would never have taken anywhere my friends would see us together, but I figured maybe she'd be good for a start, in the sexual way I mean. How naive old Jimmy was back then. What I thought I needed was experience, but all I got was aggravation, if you know what I mean.

By then I had bought my old Chevy and I thought there would be no holding me back this time. I took my pudgy little fig out for a pizza and then I took her out to a place where a narrow two-track ran down beside some railroad tracks. Even before I had stopped the car she began to protest.

"I don't know if this is such a good idea," she said. Hers was a whiny voice, just as one might expect from such a grapefruit.

"Come on," I said, putting my arm around her. "What could it hurt?"

"It's not that I'm afraid to," she protested, "but I'm just not sure you love me."

'Oh Lordy,' I thought, 'why the hell would she want to go and bring up a word like that?'

With my other hand I tried to nuzzle a way into her crotch. She was wearing bluejeans, so this was not an easy task.

At once she took a vice-grip hold of my wrist and would not let it go. "Don't," she said.

"What's the matter?" I soothed, still trying to get at least close enough to feel the warmth of that area.

"Don't," she said again, fiercely.

In fear, I drew back. It was just possible, I reasoned, that this Viking would bite a chunk out of my ear. How would I explain that to my parents? "What's the matter?" I soothed again, looking her in the eyes.

"I'm not sure you love me," she insisted.

"I'm not sure either," I retorted, "until..."

"Look," she said, taking complete charge of the situation, "either tell me you love me or take me straight home."

I took her home. "I'll be damned if I'll ever say a thing like that to someone like you," I said.

She wept all the way. Tears ran down her stodgy face and she looked like a baby-doll nightmare. When we reached her house she shouted, "You'll never know how much people love you." Then she slammed the car door and stormed away.

Her remark came as quite a surprise because, after all, I had never thought anyone even noticed me. I thought of myself as an undesirable little creep. My introverted nature, you see, kept others at arm's length, and kept me from having to deal with them. But if others did love me, then I had a special responsibility to them, didn't I?

Then my grandmother died and soon thereafter I came to my senses about things. I don't know, maybe it was just a hormonal change. Suddenly I came alive and then I was not so bashful around others.

I finally did score later, to put the matter crudely as the act itself, with a German fraulein who wanted nothing more than to snare an American husband. We met in a beer tent at a provincial rendering of the Oktoberfest festivities, and made love, using that term very loosely indeed, afterward. We were both boozy and uncertain. She went through the odd looks and motions of enticement mechanically and I was lured in, not by any real feelings of attraction, but by my own idea of how I should perform in such a situation. Later, however, we both felt like low-budget actors who had once again done something we could not be proud of. Sometimes we humans can be so stupid.

When we had finished our play she rolled over onto her stomach so as to look me straight in the eye. "Are you going to marry me and take me back to America?" she asked bluntly. Her English was almost as American as my own. She despised the German language and Germany itself. Who knows why. But even as she asked me I could detect a note of despair in her tone. She knew as well as I that we were an impossible match.

"Sure I'll take you home with me," I said brightly.

She knew I was lying and began to weep. I have never stopped feeling sorry for her and I wonder where she is today.

When I went back to where we had been sleeping, Sarah was up and thrashing her arms around. "Good Lord, it's cold," she said.

"Did you sleep at all?" I asked.

"Like a baby, I was so tired. Only once I woke up and I thought I was hugging you."

"You were."

"If I was, then I'm sorry. I didn't mean to cause you any trouble."

"We needed to stay warm," I said brusquely.

"Did it work?" she asked.

"For a while. The days when I enjoyed sleeping out on the ground are over, though."

"Me too," she said, rubbing ruefully at the muscles in her hips and thighs.

"It would be warmer if we got out on the road," I said.

"We won't get many rides at this time of day," she warned.

"At least we could walk ourselves warm."

"That's better than nothing," she said.

Having nothing to pack, we went straightaway down the hill to the road. There, in spite of what we had hoped, a biting breeze was following the cut in the mountains right down into our faces. It was sharp enough to bring weepy tears to my eyes.

How strange life is!

Yeah though I walk through the mountains with an angel, I will fear no insanity. Thy wind and Thy darkness they comfort me.

No cars came by. We were on our own.

TEN

I kept setting up in my mind, little scenarios that might bring our story to some happy conclusion. Perhaps even now Morton Toombs was being arrested, having been tracked by Interpol across Europe. Sarah could then get the treatment she so badly needed and her recovery might be miraculously quick. I would go to visit her every chance I got and we might be given the time we needed to further develop our feelings toward one another. The only trouble was, I didn't believe in any of that. Something terrible was going to happen to us, I just knew it, and there wasn't a thing either of us could do to prevent it. We were on a peculiar course that would lead, eventually, to our most singular tragedy. It only remained to play our hand out to the end, and to see what that tragedy would be.

The charcoal of night had turned a virulent blue-black, promising the dawn. The enchanted mists of Holland and Germany were behind us. The air here was crisp and clear. We plodded along the highway's edge amiably, glad for the chance to stretch our cold, stiff bones.

Hopeful scenarios aside, I truly expected at any moment that our giant nemesis would pull up alongside in a rented car and turn his big grinning face toward us. Where could we run from here? There were no trails leading up into the mountains surrounding us. The road was defined by the shear rock face on each side. We would be trapped.

When it came, the sun rose boldly, without strokes of color against the sky to forewarn us. We witnessed its presence first on the very tops of the mountains to our right, and watched as the light inched its way down toward the road. At long last we felt its welcome warmth on our faces.

Cars had begun to rush past, apparently carrying people to work. Though we put out our thumbs, no one stopped. Some of the drivers shrugged and indicated with their hands that they were turning off just ahead. It was all local traffic.

"It's such a perfect morning," Sarah said, suddenly coming awake, "I don't care if we ever get a ride."

"You seem awfully cheery this morning," I said drolly.

"Yes," she said brightly, "I guess I am."

The inside of my mouth was coated with a disgusting layer of stale mucus and my head ached dully. I did not, in short, welcome the day as she did. Sleeping on the ground did not seem to have had an adverse affect on either her spirit or her appearance. Her skin, in this light, was milky but with a tinge of pink, as if rose petals had been dipped in her coloring as she was being created, just before it dried. There was a lightness about her countenance that was, for want of a better word, angelic. She seemed to possess the very oneness of being that I lacked.

Perhaps I have not yet said enough about Sarah to make her clear in the reader's mind. In some ways, and that lightness of being was one, she seemed much younger than me. Her personality was not in the least morose, as mine sometimes is, and she possessed that awesome singleness of purpose that can be found only in the very young. The innocence of her belief in angels gave her a sweet naivete which also added to her illusion of extreme youth. I say illusion because she was only a few years younger than me.

Now that I have time to think about it, I realize this was the big difference between us. Life had not yet run her over as it had me. She had never been steam-rollered. Nor had she been worn down bit by bit, eroded over time, as I had been. She had never made compromises in order to survive. I wondered, then, how, in this day and age, she had managed to neatly elude the pitfalls of our modern time, and had managed to remain so intact. In that regard, she was still quite childlike.

There was, at that time, a fearsome struggle going on within me. (This was, of course, before I knew anything about Paragon). It seemed, then, as if the rift in my being had been created by my breaking with the construction business and the departing on this journey, but in reality that breaking off was only a symptom of the underlying illness. Now that I had traveled through half my life, I realized I had traded too much away. In order to escape the possibility of madness, I had given up those things that would have made me a viable, lively person. My fear of insanity, in short, had driven me away from my own true nature.

My entire existence had become luke warm. It was only barely tolerable. Though I had no reason to fear a fall into screaming madness, I also had no hope of ever attaining great heights. There was no risk, to be sure, and no wonder either. My days had become long unrelieved periods of boredom that I approached without pain and without joy. I plodded, (my father had once warned me of my plodding behavior), through life calmly, without commitment to its great schemes, nor with the contentment which comes from knowing one's true self. For the longest time now my soul had been in a state of continual slumber.

How does one awaken his slumbering soul? I wondered. Since childhood I had given up imagination and creativity and had taken refuge instead in the tranquil recesses of my solitude. By wrapping myself up in a builder's boisterous life, I had managed to avoid the pitfalls of my sensitive nature. Not, mind you, that I find anything wrong with working with one's hands. It was only that, in my case, I was going the wrong way. The two sides of myself, those opposite spheres of action and contemplation, were in constant opposition. And, uncertain of who I was, I was lost in the delusion of our modern times. What else could I have expected, after all?

Still, I had resisted my true calling for all those years. Mine is not an isolated case either, I have come to learn. There are many others who resist their thoughtful, solitary side in favor of the easily digested surface world. Trouble is, this tame surface, by its very nature, does not sustain. One will find nothing noble there. It is easily devoured in a single gulp, but leaves one with an unsettled, miserable feeling in the pit of the stomach. It is an empty feeling, one that makes the eater wonder what has been missed. This meal, I can tell you from experience, dear reader, leads only to disappointment.

My hope had been, in beginning this journey, to tame the insatiable beast of my inner self. His noiseless passage had gone unnoticed by all but me. I could feel him in there still, eating like a worm at my guts. The more I ignored his presence, the greater his hold on my deep entrails became. He had never been tamed, only shoved down out of sight. Only the angry, inflamed atmosphere of my interior felt his bitter shame as I passed each day uselessly, and without sparkle. "There is more for you!" he screamed, but I continued to ignore his cry.

At last a car stopped to give us a ride. In it there was an older couple: the man white-haired and leathery, the woman sandy and smiling. They both spoke excellent English.

"We're going as far as Spiez if you need a ride," the man said. "When we get there we're going to climb the mountain, Bonderspiez. You could come along with us if you like, or we could drop you in the town."

Sarah and I exchanged looks. "Well," I said to her, "it would get us off this road for a while."

"I've been worried about being out here," she said. "We're so... unprotected."

"We'd like to climb along with you," I told the man, sealing the bargain as we got into the car.

"You don't have backpacks?" the woman asked, turning to look over her seat.

"No," I said shortly, "we don't." I didn't want her to start asking a lot of questions.

"We're traveling light," Sarah told her, feigning gaiety.

We drove far up from the valley floor, some three miles beyond the town, and then the man parked the car and we began walking up the path. The way was muddy and slippery. The wind was chilly and clouds were coming in. One moment we could see for miles across the ranges and the small villages nestled in their valleys below, and the next moment the clouds were upon us and we could scarcely see the path in front of us.

Up top they shared hot chocolate with us from a Thermos. "You should have jackets," the woman admonished.

"We lost them," Sarah explained. "We're going to buy some things once we get to Thun."

By the time we came back into the town of Spiez, it was late afternoon. We headed out onto the road but no cars stopped for us. They continued to whiz by as it grew dark. Then it began to rain. There was no place to take refuge among the rocks along the road. Complete darkness fell.

"What do you think of me now that I've led you into a life on the road?" Sarah asked grimly. Rain was running down her face. She was shivering.

"I've been in the rain before," I said gruffly. "In the army."

"Oh yes, I forgot. It's just that... I never had been. Never before last week, I mean."

"Angels don't experience rain, I suppose."

"We don't," she said quickly. "They don't," she corrected sadly.

"What's it like then, being an angel?"

"It's a constant state of pleasure."

"This world can never live up to that," I said. "There's pain here and lots of it."

"So I've noticed. But you know what, when I was the way I was before, when I was an angel, I never knew the difference."

"The bliss got old, is that it?"

"There was no way to tell the bliss from anything else."

"Suffering heightens your pleasure, does it?"

"It seems to, in some ways. There is no way to truly appreciate a thing until there has been something else."

"I'll pass on the pain thing, myself. I've had plenty already. If I had my way, I'd never experience another minute of it in this life."

We continued to walk. Sarah shook her head slowly. "Haven't you already been hiding from it all this time?"

"What, pain? You're damned right I have been. You'd have to be nuts to welcome pain with open arms."

"Not welcome it," she said, "but to work through it, knowing that it is part of life. Don't you think that life is something more than just keeping ourselves entertained?"

"You're the philosopher," I said.

"We have to pay for everything we gain in this life, and pain is part of the payment."

"I've never gained on anything," I objected.

"You're gaining now."

"Then I should quit right now."

"What a coward you are!" she exclaimed, turning to look at me.

The word stung. I have always lived with this nagging fear that sooner or later someone was going to find me out. And now, here she had done it. I had let her in. She was too close. My first instinct, naturally, was to push her away.

"Leave me alone," I said, taking as cold a tone as I could muster.

"Are you going to spend your whole life alone, then?"

"What I do with my life is up to me now, isn't it?"

"What are you so afraid of?" she asked, though gently.

"I'm not afraid of anything."

"You are afraid of something. I just have never been able to figure out what," she persisted.

"You don't know me at all," I countered.

"But I do know you," she said. "I know you, perhaps, better than you know yourself."

"You poor, deluded thing," I scoffed. "No one can know me. I've made a career of it."

"I know you," she said. "No one could know you as I do."

We must have been quite a sight, walking along in the dark, the rain harping down, ranting at each other in this manner. Perhaps the adversity of our situation was causing this sudden dissention between us, but I think we understood very well that it was also caused by our fear. We were afraid to go further together, and so we were both holding back.

After a long pause I said, "You think you know so much about me, but you don't. If you knew anything at all about me, you'd know there are some places you just shouldn't tread."

"I won't ruffle you," she said. "For now. But don't worry, you'll change."

We walked along in silence again for a few minutes. She was wrong, of course. I was too old to change now. I liked my life too well. I had made up an alternative character for myself, the one I played off against the world to give them a certain illusion, while the real me operated in secret behind the veil.

Did she suspect all this? The very idea that she might frightened me. I knew I could never cross that line, exposing the real me. No, the secret spy of my youth would never allow that. Life is too cruel, I had learned. In order to open myself up to her I would become vulnerable to all kinds of ridicule and pain. It simply was not worth the risk.

It may be, as Sarah had suggested, that we have been sent here to live, to experience all that the world has to throw at us, but I knew I had no capacity for such living. Though it is true that I have never sought trouble or danger or adversity in any of its myriad forms, I must confess that each time I have been confronted by these things (the loneliness, despair, a ruthless enemy), I have grown, often in spite of my best efforts to the contrary. The disruptions, the explosions, the uproars that I have endured here-to-for have been mild, probably, when compared to the trials of others, but to me they have seemed terrible enough. I wondered, trembling along in my fear, what I might face if I actually did choose the path Sarah was proposing. Might not every power in heaven and on earth conspire to remove me from that path? Was I not better off to avoid that way at all cost?

Oh why had I ever left my kind home behind. Why had I ventured out here beyond my own horizons? Oh that I were back in Michigan right now, pursuing my limited but attainable dreams, and facing my minuscule but surmountable daily dilemmas, and working and living alongside those people I neither loved nor hated, but whom I at least knew.

Such were my thoughts at that time.

Sarah, on the other hand, seemed perfectly content to be walking along in the rain and cold, as if she could see purpose where it seemed quite obvious to me there was none. "Something will open up," she said, "you'll see."

I do not often lose my way, gentle reader. Since childhood I have had an innate, almost infallible sense of direction. That sense of direction, I believe, is an extension of my reasoning abilities. Because I reject that which may cause pandemonic disturbances within me, I am better able to control my place in the external world as well. But now, since dark, everything around me had become increasingly unfamiliar. This was not, I am convinced, simply the result of my travels in a strange new land. I had been drawn, somehow, into a world of extreme uncertainty.

In a way, Sarah had become my guiding angel. When I remarked this fact, she merely laughed. But she continued to lead the way. I followed docilely.

Could it be that I had somehow advanced beyond myself, just as my boss had done those seven months earlier? I might already be mad, I thought. (How does one determine such a thing about one's self?) Free thinking takes a certain courage, you see. I did want to awaken, to absorb learning, and to breathe free at last. I wanted to break free of the bonds that were holding me fast, but I also wanted to maintain my secure boundaries. I was clinging, in short, to that reality which had sustained me so well in the past.

Trouble was, looking back now, I see that I was like a snake about to shed his skin. The old skin had always served me quite well, so I was loath to be done with it. But a new, better one was emerging, and there was no holding it back. Once the process of shedding had begun, the minute I had broken with my old construction job and had embarked upon this journey, my second skin had begun irreversibly displacing the old one. Already, though I did not yet know it, my old life had split along the back and I was bulging out of it impatiently. Even as I attempted to hold onto what had been, the new was inexorably thrusting itself upon me.

For the longest time I had expressed nothing of my true feelings. I had hidden my thoughts and concerns from even the gods, because I feared their retribution. In hidden pools, these feelings had become bitter wells. My fine-tuned deceptions had become so automatic, it seems, that I was deceiving even myself.

Now, however, I found myself in a situation I was unable to avoid. I was compelled to follow these events to their proper conclusion, whatever that might be. There was no way out.

My only companion on this journey, as it turned out, was Sarah. A woman who thought herself to be an angel. She seemed in complete control of herself, and of the situation about us, even when I was not. This was uncanny. I am used to being in charge.

I looked at her. Her face suggested intelligence and radiated hope. She was beauty personified.

In the darkness, I felt my way along uncertainly. Inwardly, I was stricken with panic and agony. I needed rest. I needed a wayside inn of some kind. A place to stop and reassess the situation I now found myself in.

There was no such place nearby. The rain did not relent. Darkness seeped into my very soul.

At last, however, a small earthen track did open up on our right, running up into the emptiness of the night. "Where do you think it will lead?" I asked Sarah. I could hear the weariness in my own voice.

"There's only one way to find out," she said.

Tears were close behind my eyes. I had not been so exhausted; cold, wet, hungry, and thirsty in a long, long, time. If we got off the main road, there was no telling where we would end up. Yet, if we continued on in the way we had been going, we might never find shelter at all. Sarah seemed as unconcerned about all this as ever. Her path, whatever it might be, seemed never in doubt.

"One way is as good as the other to you, isn't it?" I said in an accusing tone.

"They all lead to the same place," she said with a shrug.

"They all lead to death," I said fatalistically.

"They all lead to life," she countered.

I was too tired to argue with her. For some reason I cannot now fathom, I opted for the dirt track.

"Up this way?" she asked.

I nodded.

Perhaps we'd find an overhanging rock where we could rest out of the rain, I thought. My muscles ached, my feet were sore, and I was so tired I almost could not keep my eyes open. We crossed a narrow bridge that spanned what seemed to be a bottomless void.

Then, abruptly, the rain ceased. I caught my breath. I had been shuffling along mindlessly, mouth slightly open, as when snoring, and Sarah had been leading the way up into the hills. We proceeded around a shoulder of the mountain and there, on my left, jutting from the solid rock face, was a metal pipe spouting water. We took turns drinking from it. The water was cold and pure.

When she had taken her turn, Sarah turned to me and said, "The water is here. When you need it most, you will find the water."

"What is that supposed to mean?" I snapped. "This pipe has been here all along. Don't try to make out like it just materialized."

"Of course it has been here," she said, "but we haven't."

I gave up trying to reason out what she was saying. What good was it doing me? One never wins such an argument.

We continued around the bend in the trail with the rock shoulder on our left. Then the view opened up and there was a little village below, its lights bright against the darkness. The hour was late and the town was mostly asleep. I glanced over at Sarah and she was smiling happily. This was all reassurance for her, but it was unsettling for me.

There was a small hotel on the first corner we came to; white with dark wooden beams. I rang the buzzer beside the door and after a time someone, a man, came. With a sad shrug of his shoulders he let us know that the place was full.

"What are we going to do now?" I lamented. "We'll freeze to death before morning, wet as we are."

"We'll be alright," Sarah said.

Before I could say anything more, (and be sure gentle reader that I was about to say something cynical and defeatist in nature), a portly man came around the corner of the building holding a piece of birthday cake in a cardboard box.   "You two look hungry," he said in English.   His breath was thick with alcohol. "Here, have a piece."

The owner of the hotel ducked back inside.   Sarah and I took a piece of cake and split it between us.

"It's got rum in it," the man said in his bellowing voice.

"Thankyou," I said.   "It's very good."

"This is my girlfriend."   He stepped aside and introduced a nice-looking young lady.   "She's German.   She doesn't speak English."

The girl smiled nicely. I did not, then, understand the interconnectedness of all things, so you can imagine my general state of confusion about what was happening.

"This place is full?" the man said.

"Yes, it is. Do you know of another hotel nearby?"

"There is no other," he said.   "But I'll let you sleep in my car tonight if you promise me one thing. Promise not to steal my car."

"Really?" Sarah said.   "That would be great.   We're so wet and cold..."

"You can run the heater. I'll leave you the keys. Get in."

The car was a Renault. He drove us up into the hills above the town where he had an apartment.   When we all got out the man laid the seats down for us. "You run the heater," he said, handing me the keys. "Do whatever you like only, please, don't steal my car."

"I won't steal it," I promised. Then, apparently satisfied, he and his girlfriend went up the stairs to his apartment.

ELEVEN

By this time I was becoming more and more convinced that I had made a poor choice in leaving my former life behind and in setting out on this wild and dangerous journey. There was no way for me, then, to comprehend the intricate patterns of destiny that were at work. Now, as never before, I felt I had been abandoned to my fate by an unconcerned God in an uncaring universe. My uncertain future ran on mindlessly before me in a series of serpentine twistings, never revealing itself clearly.

Though we had found refuge here, in this man's car, I was still wet and miserable and unable to sleep. Sarah, on the other hand, drifted off as if she had not a care in the world. For some time I agonized over my recent past and my immediate future.

What was to become of us?

I simply could not figure out what I was doing there. My life had, in the past, been withdrawn and retiring. I was not prepared to face an uncertain future filled with deadly obstacles. I felt exceptionally tired and old, and yet I could not sleep.

Should I not think of myself first? Right now I could slip out of here and be on my way happy and free in no time. I could return to Michigan any time I wanted, and get my old job back. Or any old construction job, come to that. What was this woman to me?

Even as I thought these things, however, I knew very well that there could never be any going back for me. Somehow I had traversed a road that was even now crumbling behind me. The way behind was not negotiable. Only the way ahead was clear, as far as I could see along it, in any case.

At some point I must have slept because the next thing I knew I was dreaming. I had entered some kind of vast symbolic work of fiction. The landscape seemed boxy and half finished, as if it had been sketched and never completed. There was something ironic about the way the trees held themselves. Monstrous boulders lay here and there, unconcerned. The sky was only partially colored blue. The rest was white as paper. I had become lost in this disturbing landscape full of distortions and contorted mosaics,

106

and the road was falling away behind me with every step I took. I was busily trying to determine my present position, but there seemed no way to do this. The map I was carrying was old and creased many times, so much so that it was virtually useless to me.

The further I walked along the trail I was on, the less I understood about my course. Who knew what prospects lay ahead for me, and who knew what trials. To make matters worse, it was growing dark. It was not easy to distinguish anything in the faltering light. I was sure that in another hour I would be completely disoriented in this emptiness.

Then Sarah flew down out of the unfinished heavens. Her wings were made of some glowing, transparent material. I was so astonished to see her there I said, "Where did you come from?"

"Does that matter?" she answered. "The only thing that matters is that I'm here now, and that you need my help."

"I do need your help," I admitted, "because I don't know where I am or where I'm going."

"That's because you've come a long way off the path."

"I thought I was going right," I said. Now that I looked closely, however, I was surprised to notice that I was not on a road at all, but lost in some thorny plain with an uneven surface.

"You missed a turning some way back," she said.

I turned to look back, but saw that there was a deep canyon between me and my past. There was no way to go back. "How do I get back?" I asked her.

"Silly, there's no going back now. Not from here."

"That's odd," I said. "I had the feeling that I was supposed to go back."

"Sorry," she said. "We'll just have to keep looking ahead. That's why I'm here, you know. To help you along your way."

"What happened to your wings?" I looked closely at her, at the place where her wings had been. They had vanished.

In surprise and fear Sarah looked over her shoulder and saw that her wings were, indeed, missing. She began to sob. "Oh what a sacrifice. What a sacrifice."

"You did that for me, didn't you?" I said.

She nodded, unable to speak now through her tears. After a bit she said, "I haven't much hope of anything now."

"Don't say that," I said, taking up her challenge. "We're in this together. We have at least that much."

I came to myself abruptly. The sun was tasting the eastern horizon. For a long moment I lay there, still cramped in that front seat, and thought about my dream. Its meaning was not too hard to figure out, to be sure, but I was not at all sure, then, that I believed in the meanings of dreams.

At last I reached over and touched Sarah's shoulder to awaken her. "What?" she said, sitting up and blinking her eyes.

"It's morning," I said.

"Thank God," she said.

"Why do you say it like that?"

"I was having a nightmare. Toombs caught us. He injected us with some kind of immobilizing drug. We couldn't move. He was telling us all about hell just as he was getting ready to take us there."

"It was just a dream," I said. I did not tell her about my dream.

"Just a dream, yes," she said. "But also reality. There is no direct connection between our dreams and reality, it's true, but there is 'a' connection."

The morning was still and majestic. Since we were up so early, I slipped the keys of the Renault under the mat and we walked into town. We had a light breakfast at an early restaurant and then, when the stores opened, we bought new backpacks and sleeping bags, and the various other items needed to fill them for our continuing journey. Then we took a circuitous route to the border. We certainly did not want Morton Toombs to find us again and so far we had done well at eluding him. Still, Sarah insisted that he would find us sooner or later.

"What makes you so sure?" I asked her. "Does he have some kind of angelic nose or something."

"Yes, something like that. It won't do you any good to make fun of me, though. Let's just pretend I'm right, since that's the safest thing."

I had to agree with her logic there, so we took precautions not to be spotted along the normal routes.

Out on the highway we were picked up almost at once by an American shoe salesman in a Chevy Impala, which was big and odd next to the other cars on the road. "I had it shipped over specially," he said. "I can't stand to drive a small car." He drove at a screeching pace down through the mountains and left us alive, thankfully, near the Italian border.

While we were standing alongside the road watching the Chevy speed away, two young Texans pulled up in a grape purple microbus. "Hey buddy," one of them called over. "You two headed into Italy?"

"We sure are."

"Well hop in then." He swung open the side door and we crawled ourselves in amongst the mess of their living quarters. There was a mattress under there somewhere, under clothes and cooking pots and blankets and camping gear.

As we came down toward the border near Como, we overheard the conversation between the two boys up front:

"Did you hide the stash?"

"Yeah, man."

"Where'd you hide it?"

"Where they'll never find it."

Sarah and I looked at each other uneasily. That's all we'd need, to wind up in an Italian jail cell.

We were met at the border by guards with submachine guns. They motioned us out of the van and then began poking through the things in the back. I wondered if they would call for the dogs. While they were at it, I nervously took some coins out of my pants pocket and began to jingle them back and forth between my cupped hands. One of the guards turned to give me an irritated look. In my rush to halt what I was doing, a quarter popped out of my hand and fell on the pavement. The guard picked it up and examined it closely. What did he expect to find? I wondered.

"George Washington," he said. His eyes met mine. What was he driving at?

"Yes," I said uncertainly.

He pointed at the face of the coin and smiled. "George Washington."

"That's right," I said. I handed him another coin, a penny. "Abraham Lincoln."

"Lincoln," he beamed.

I handed over more coins. "Souvenirs," I said.

"Souvenirs?" He cocked his head to one side.

"For Christmas."

"Ah, Christmas."

"For your kids. For your children."

He smiled, accepted the coins, and then called something over to the other guards. They all backed away on his orders and then he waved us through into Italy.

"That was a hell of a nice move," one of the Texans said, smiling at me in the rearview mirror.

"That was smooth," said the other. "That had to be the cheapest bribe in the history of the world."

"Yeah, what was that, about fifty cents?"

They both burst out laughing at the idea. "You sure saved us, man."

"You see," Sarah whispered, "there is never anything to fear. We're going the right way."

"Great," I muttered. "That's just what I always wanted, to help some guys smuggle drugs across the border.

The town of Como lay at the south end of Lake Como and was surrounded by mountains. From there we headed west, skirting the Alps, to the town of Bergamo, where the Texans dropped us off. They were heading south from there, they said.

The lower part of the town was the industrial area with cement factories and textile mills, while the upper part, the Bergamo Alta, was the old section.

We took the funicular railway up the hill and spent the better part of the day wandering the narrow labyrinthian streets from the Palazzo della Ragione to the ancient walls and bastions built by Venitians four hundred years earlier. Then we hiked out of town and camped near a lake as storm clouds again rose overhead. Everything grew still and muggy. We bought some bread and cheese and wine and shared a meal just before dark. Hoping to avoid the rainfall, we stretched our sleeping bags out under a pine tree.

As we lay down to get our sleep, I rolled over onto one elbow and looked at Sarah. She looked at me for a long moment and then said, "What is it?" in an embarrassed way.

"I was just thinking that I have told you quite a bit about myself already, but you really haven't told me anything at all about yourself."

"I've told you everything," she objected, rolling up onto her elbow so that she could look evenly across at me.

"You haven't told me anything I want to know. You haven't told me where you were born, or who your parents were, or did you have any brothers or sisters."

After a long moment during which she searched my eyes for some meaning beyond my words she said, "I'm sorry, I thought I had made that clear. There was none of that for me. I was not born at all. Not in the way you mean. My essence was created at the beginning of time, just as yours was, but I have never been born in the flesh. Not until now, anyway."

"So you have no mother and father, is that what you're saying?" I was not angry at her response, as I had been before. I was still trying to make some sense of her whole story. After my dream of the night before, anything seemed possible.

"My Father is God Himself, and my mother is the Holy Spirit. I have qualities of each of them."

"You have no home, then?"

"My home is in heaven."

"But you're on earth now," I said.

"Then my home is with you. I know of no other home."

I leaned forward and kissed her lips. She kissed me back. After a moment she eased down so that her shoulder was once again on the ground, and pulled me down with her, her left hand resting on the back of my neck. I felt as if I were falling.

When I had the chance to catch my breath I said, "You are always going to be a mystery to me, aren't you?"

"We are all mysteries to each other," she said. "But I have the feeling we're going to come to know each other as well as any two people can."

We spent some time looking into each others' eyes, and then we kissed again. I knew I wanted her, but I knew also that I could not have her here, out in the open in the middle of this campground. Eventually we snuggled against each other and went to sleep.

Later that night I woke up with a start. My skin was itching and here and there I felt hot pinpricks of pain. What was going on here? I unzipped my bag and fumbled around and found my flashlight. In its beam I found that I was being invaded by tiny red spiders. They had been coming down out of the tree and were biting me fiercely all over.

With all the commotion I was causing, Sarah woke up. She too came out of her bag in a hurry. They were eating her alive as well.

"What are they?" she said, swatting at the skin on her arms.

"Spiders," I said. "Come on."

She followed me down to the lake where we splashed ourselves clean of these uninvited guests. Then, just as we got back up to our camp site, it began to rain. There were a few sprinkles at first, and then the clouds burst. We scurried around packing our gear, but within a few minutes everything was drenched.

"At least the spiders are gone," Sarah said.

"I'm not in the mood for any more rain," I said dourly.

We dragged all of our gear over to the outhouse where we spent the rest of the night sitting up under its overhanging roof. "I'll never get to sleep now," I said.

"Who would have thought it would rain this much here?"

The light from a mercury lamp on a pole was shining directly into my eyes. Rain water was pouring off the roof, causing the light to seem to jump back and forth in a distorted way.

"My whole world is out of balance," I said after watching the odd play of the water and the light for some time.

"It's a positive nightmare, isn't it?"

"There doesn't seem to be any place for me anymore. I don't know who I am. I don't know where I'm going."

"It's the same for me," she said glumly. "Maybe that's why we have come together like this."

"Do you think so?"

"It's a possibility."

I was having trouble judging her mood. Unlike the characters one finds in novels, there was no way to neatly compartmentalize her emotions. They were quick and variable, and often overlapping.

"What do you think about when I kiss you?" I asked. "Do you like it. It's hard for me to tell."

"Of course I like it," she said. "What did you think?"

"I thought maybe you were just playing along."

"I'm surprised you would think that. We don't have to act like innocents, you know."

"No?"

"None of us are innocent any more."

"Except maybe you."

"Not even me. I'm no angel. Not now."

"I see."

"I wonder if you do. We've both made a break with the past, you know. I'm doing my best to adapt to the changes. Are you?"

"I'm trying," I said. "I'm afraid, that's all." I don't know why I admitted this to her.

"We all have secret sources of power that will see us through."

"Are you my secret power?" I asked.

"I'm hardly a secret now, am I."

"Would you mind if I kissed you again?" I said.

"I've been kissing you in my mind already."

I kissed her. When I drew away and looked at her face, it was bathed in eerie shadows from the mercury light.

"What's wrong?" she asked.

"I don't really know you at all," I said.

"Don't you?"

The fact was, I did know her. I knew her through and through. There was no doubt about what our future together would be. That was, perhaps, the scariest thing of all.

In spite of what I had said, we did get some sleep in the early hours of the morning. The rain continued and we slumped together, pulling our new sleeping bags up around us. Nothing was familiar now. Even our gear was brand new. We had very little of our past with us.

In the morning we hung our sleeping bags out to dry. The rain had stopped some time while we slept. Several hours passed.

"When we get to Brecia, we probably should take a bus over to Venice," I said. "The more we can keep off the road, the better."

"I agree," she said. "We have to take every precaution to stay out of sight. Staying in out-of-the-way places like this campground is a good idea."

"Do you really think he'll be able to track us, wherever we go?"

"Yes, I do. He's been following me all along. I don't know how this will be any different."

"How does he do it, do you suppose?"

"I know how he does it.   An angel gives off a certain aura.
You can't sense it, of course, but he can.   There must be a residue
left on me, even though I'm no longer an angel."

"Then why can't you sense when he is near?"

"I don't know," she said.   "I must have lost my powers when
I made the transformation.   I'm only human now."

"And he, Toombs, is still something more than human?"

"Oh yes.   He is not human at all.   He was sent here to take
me back with him.   It's his angelic mission."

"It seems odd to me, to be speaking of angels from hell.   I
always thought of angels as good."

"Just like everything else, angels can be good or bad."

Once our sleeping bags had dried in the warm sun of that
morning, we headed out onto the road again.   It was there, some
minutes later, I noticed that my passport was missing.

"I don't know where it could be," I said, vainly searching my
pockets.   "It was here last night.   I remember seeing it."

"Maybe you dropped it along the road here," Sarah said.

We searched back along the road and even back to the
campground, but we could not find it.

"I'll have to report it lost at the next police station," I said
at last, giving up.

"That's the only thing left to do," Sarah agreed.

On the road we were picked up right away by a man driving
a large Mercedes truck.   He was going to Verona so we decided
to ride that far with him.   He agreed to drop us off in front of the
police station there.

We passed through Brecia with its old town surrounded by
fresh gardens and the Torre dell-Orologio clock tower.   Then we
were on to Verona, which is on the Adige river and is noted for
its having been the setting for Romeo and Juliet.

The driver knew right where he was going, though it did not
take long for us to get turned around.   He crossed the Adige on the
Ponte Catena and followed the river along the San Giorgio, but
after that it was impossible to keep up with the various roads and
turnings.

After some minutes the driver pulled over and let us out.
We found ourselves in front of the tall police station, so we went
inside.   None of the carabiniere spoke more than a word or two of

English and we, of course, spoke no Italian. It did not take long, however, to get our point across.

Sorrowfully, the chief of the carabiniere shook his head. There was no way, apparently, for him to issue me a passport. He could, he described to us as best he could, issue me a paper that would serve as a passport. I accepted his paper, stamped and signed officially, and thanked him.

As we turned to leave the building, we saw Morton Toombs blocking the doorway of the station. He had a wide grin on his face and called, "Greetings, friends, it has been a long time, has it not."

I could feel Sarah tense beside me, but I was not afraid. We were in a police station, after all. What did we have to fear from the likes of him as long as we were in here?

"What are you doing here?" I said, taking a threatening step forward. "Why don't you leave us alone."

"Be careful," Sarah cautioned from behind me.

Toombs took a step forward as well. He was preparing himself for the attack. "That girl is mine," he said. His voice seemed to take on an other-worldly resonance.

A young carabiniere in his smart uniform came in the door behind Toombs. Startled, the big man turned and lashed out. A startling blat of blood hit the wall. The young officer flew back and then fell to the floor.

There was shouting. Shots were fired. Everything happened so fast I could not tell exactly what was going on.

"Let's go," Sarah said. She took hold of my hand and urged me toward the door. "There is nothing we can do."

TWELVE

As we came out of the building and down the steps in front, I found that my heart was lunging inside me. Adrenalin was rushing through my veins. I seemed unable to breathe fast enough to meet my needs. Sarah was still urging me along quickly.

"I'm not very good in confrontations," I said.

"That's not a bad thing in this case."

"He really hurt that young policeman..."

"He killed him, I'm quite sure."

"... I should have done something to help him."

Several more shots were fired within the building. From here they sounded like dull pops.

"You couldn't have helped him," Sarah said. "Toombs would have killed you too."

"Well, in any case, he's in the hands of the police now."

"He'll just kill them all, and then he'll be after us again. They won't stop him."

"I can't believe that." I felt numb all over. My blood had been released. There was no panic. Everything was serene.

At the corner Sarah hailed a taxi. We jumped in and ordered him to the bus station. From there we took the next bus out. It was headed west toward Vicenza.

Once we had settled in our seats, I began to shake all over. I felt like crying. All of the tension of the last twenty minutes suddenly caught up with me like a boom. The tension settled in my jaw and shoulders and in the muscles of my thighs.

"Are you alright?" Sarah asked.

I nodded and tried to take a deep breath. The air came into my lungs in jerky spurts. My lungs heaved up and down sporadically. "I should have done something," I said at last.

"There was nothing you could have done. If we'd have stayed, we would be dead too."

"What makes you so sure he's killed them all. What kind of weapon does he carry?"

"He is a weapon. I told you that before. He doesn't need

the square mouth, the close-cropped head, the massive dimensions and the burning black eyes I had always witnessed in my worst nightmares. His whole being seemed to be boiling in sulfuric properties. His body seemed to be straining to get out of its skin.

Still, even knowing his great power and suspecting his great capacity for evil, I was not afraid. A certain calmness had descended over me. I felt curious, more than anything. Curious about why I was here at hell's gate, and curious about what I would find beyond it. Was it as Dante had written?

"Why have you brought us here?" I asked him.

"You have brought yourselves here," Toombs replied. "Your own curiosity has led you into my home. I am to conduct your tour."

"But I..."

"Don't worry, you have nothing to fear by being here. It is not yet your time."

"... I'm the least curious man I know," I said, continuing my objection.

"Oh that may have been true at one time. That was true until last month, in fact. You had your head in the sand alright. But now you've begun your inquiries, haven't you?"

"I hadn't realized where it would lead."

"As I told you, there is no reason to hesitate. You have a free passage in, and out again. We will not attempt to detain you."

"Why should I believe you?" I asked.

"Shall we begin our little tour?" he said impatiently. "Talking will get us nowhere."

"Don't follow him," Sarah said.

"Shut up you little bitch. You've had your chance. You haven't shown him anything. Now he wants to see the other side."

"You can't talk to me that way," she protested.

"The hell I can't. You're on my home turf now. Why don't you let him make up his own mind. That's all he wants, isn't that right Jimmy my boy?"

"Well I..."

He didn't let me finish. "Women," he said in disgust. "They'll poison your mind. A man has to see for himself, doesn't he?"

"I guess we do," I agreed.

Without another word on that subject he turned and made his way up the street into his realm. I followed him and, making no further protest, Sarah tagged after me. It was not long, however, before she began to act strangely. She went up to each door as we passed and banged on it with her little fist. 'Banging on the doors of hell,' I thought. 'What is the meaning of this?'

Then, aloud I said, "What are you doing?"

"We have to get some help."

"Do you need help?"

"We need to find a doctor."

"A doctor. Are you sick?"

Then we plunged back down into the lost streets of that dark night of the soul. All around us ugly squat toads were moving restlessly. Wild birds were screeching somewhere ahead in the distance. (These turned out to be Harpies, fighting over the leaves of trees they wanted to eat).

Once I had regathered my mind, I called ahead to Toombs. "There seems to be a conspicuous absence of fallen angels here. Could it be that Heaven is prevailing after all?"

Toombs turned to look directly at me. "Of course that would be one very possible explanation."

"Is there another?"

"It is equally as possible that they are all above, on your good earth, doing whatever tasks have been assigned them," he said with a simple shrug. He did not seem to care whether I believed him or not. This, of course, made him all the more believable.

"What kinds of tasks might those be," I said, "if they are, indeed, above."

"They would be tasks similar to mine."

"What exactly is your task?"

"Ah, you still need to ask. Your reason never strays far beyond words, does it, friend?"

"Could you answer the question, please?"

"It is just as your girl there has supposed all along. We are becoming very good at trapping risen angels, and bringing them back here, where they belong."

"What happens to them when they get here?"

"They are held in captivity until they recognize the one true way."

"The true way?"

"The one true way is the one that leads to the Great One, Satan himself. There is no other way."

"Don't listen to him," Sarah whispered. "Whatever he says, don't listen. His words twist everything, remember that."

"Quiet, you simpering bitch. Life here is not as you believe. This is a good place. A place of sensual delights. Unlike the sterile silence of your heaven."

Sarah began to object, but the big man raised his hand and shouted, "Silence." As soon as he spoke that word it was as if Sarah had lost her tongue. Though she opened her mouth, no sound came out.

"You have no power here," he said. Then to me, "Some people talk too much."

"I'll be the first to admit," I said, "I don't know which way to think about all this."

"That's why you have come here, so you can decide for yourself. I think you'll find that hell, for people like us, is very much like life on earth. Except here, my friend, we have infinitely more power."

"Is it all about power, then? I thought hell was punishment."

"Dante-esque clap trap," he snorted. "Some are punished, as you say, but not those of us who are strong. We are Satan's chosen."

"You keep saying 'us'..."

"You can be one of us," he said with a libidinous wink. "You too can be here, in the halls of power."

Sarah grasped my upper arm between her two hands, but I pulled away brusquely. It was becoming tiresome having her hanging on me all the time.

Again she went up to a door and pounded on it. She was still looking for a doctor, I supposed. None of her actions made any sense. If I had come to learn about this other world, this world of opposite power, what could it hurt? The more I knew on the subject, the better off I'd be, I was quite sure.

"You said some of the risen angels are held captive..."

"Only the ones who do not convert. Foolish, really. We all serve a master. What difference does it make which one? We're all only faithful servants."

"But... (I should not have asked), "I don't see any of those captive angels about."

Toombs stamped his foot. At first I thought he was protesting my asking the question. Then I followed his eyes downward. "In the cement," he said.

"In the cement?" I did not at first understand.

"We mix them in the cement used to build our roads. None ever escape."

"Then, we're walking on them right this minute?" I stepped off to the side.

"Don't worry about offending them. It's their punishment, you see. Those who have risen so high must now lay there while we tread on them. Just punishment, wouldn't you say?"

Oddly, what he said did make a kind of back-handed sense. Still, I did not know if I wanted to be walking on Sarah's brothers and sisters, no matter what. "Are they never released?" I asked.

"Of course they are. Some are released every day. They have but to pledge their allegiance to their rightful King, the Prince of Darkness, and they fly up out of the roadway complete and unharmed. It's quite a spectacle."

"I can imagine it is."

The big man turned back to his task of leading us through the serpentine twistings of the streets of hell. "Ahead here," he said, "we have those who were violent against their neighbors and beyond them is the Park of the Suicides."

I caught my breath. That tiny park with its several trees, is where the noise from the birds or, as I was about to learn, Harpies, was emanating. I knew about this park from Dante. The leaves trapped the souls of those who had committed suicide, and the Harpies ate those leaves. All of this has a special, horrible, place in my heart.

"Your father committed suicide, didn't he?"

Sadly, I nodded. "Is he here?" I asked, against my own wishes. In truth, I was afraid to know.

"He's here, in one of these trees," Toombs affirmed. "But he doesn't have to be, you know."

"How do you mean?"

"Those of us with power can have things as we wish," he said.

"You know what I wish..." I cut myself short.

When I did not continue, Toombs cocked his head to one side and gave me a sly smile. "What do you wish?" I had the idea that he already knew. That might have been a ploy, however, to get me to talk freely.

"Nothing," I said at last. I did not want to make him privy to my regrets and to my recurrent dream. It was an odd little dream and for a long time I had not been able to make out its significance.

In the dream I am confronted by two knights on horseback, a white knight and a black knight. I have only a long staff with which to defend myself against their lances. The black knight is first. He charges his horse at me and lowers his lance. At the last possible moment I leap aside and, using my staff, pin his lance against a tree trunk, breaking it. The white knight, seeing his companion so easily defeated, turns his horse onto a lane off to my left, and disappears from sight.

I did not want to think about the dream now, and I certainly did not want to share it, or its many possible meanings, with anyone.

Beyond the Park of the Suicides we came upon the third level of the seventh circle of Dante's 'Inferno'. Here were those who had sinned by committing unnatural acts, just as I had imagined them, but here also was another group I had never expected to find in the underworld.

"Why are these people here?" I asked Toombs, still reeling in my surprise.

"They, too, are reaping their just rewards," he replied.

"But, they're writers!"

"They're writers and editors and publishers and critics. Among them you will find others as well. There are painters and sculptors and musicians..."

"What are they doing here? If I recall, this is the area reserved for unnatural acts. Wasn't that it - Acts against Nature."

"Acts against Nature and Art," Toombs corrected. "Dante missed that part too, but of course our master, His Satanic Majesty, did not miss it."

"Then you mean that they are here..."

"They are here because they sold out, to use your modern terminology. Every one of those before you had the chance to create something really special, something truly great, but they turned to lesser projects to fulfill their own desires. Such a pity, too."

"They betrayed their talent, then, is that what you're saying?"
I was still trying to get this clear in my mind.

"Exactly so. Their talents demanded greatness of them, but
they were not up to the task. They traded their talents for money
or popularity, or sexual favors. That sort of thing. None created the
art that had been reserved for them to create. Now humankind
must do without those contributions. More's the pity, wouldn't you
say?"

I scarcely dared ask my next question. Finally, taking a deep
breath to brace myself, I did ask it. "What is their punishment?"

"Can't you imagine what it must be?" he said. "Everyone
who comes here gets the punishment that suitably fits the sin. In
their case, they are forced to constantly write or compose or paint
trite entertainments that are far below their capacities. Then they
must display them to each other, and receive praises for that which
they know to be substandard. In their turn, they must praise the
works of others, though it too is trash. Since each knows better,
they are constantly tormented by their own poor creations, and by
the works of others. This goes on for all eternity."

"That's terrible," I protested in a frightened whisper.

"No more terrible than depriving humankind of their talents,
my dear friend."

"Do they never get to see a classic work again?"

"Never," he said.

"The punishment fits the sin," I reflected.

"Always."

"Then, what about you? You don't seem to be paying any
penalty here. What is your punishment?"

He gave me a curious look, but then shrugged and said, "I
have told you already, a being of power has it different."

Sarah again tried to say something, but found it impossible.

"As long as I continue to do my good works up there, on
your sweet earth, I will continue to be a being of power. We are
allowed to come and go as we wish, you see. We escape all
punishment as long as we keep our master happy."

"But what of God?" I protested. "Doesn't He have a say
about who is cast into hell?"

Toombs laughed. "The tormented soul finds its own way.
But enough of that; there is much yet for you to see."

Everything was just as I had pictured it while reading Dante's book. There were those, in the eighth circle, who were smeared with shit, and those whose feet were afire, and those whose heads were set on backward, so that their tears flowed down the crack of their buttocks. Simon the Sorcerer was there, just as Dante had predicted. (He was the one who wanted to buy the power of the Holy Spirit from Peter in Acts 8: 9-24). There were those, also, who boiled in pitch, and those who wore robes of lead, and Caiaphas himself, pinned to the floor of hell with stakes. And there were the souls that ran shrieking through the flames.

"Even their shadows pain them," Toombs explained.

Then, as we continued through the tangled streets of that night, we saw, (just as I had seen in my mind's eye while reading), the thieves trying to steal back their bodies, and the sinners clinging on the brink of this level (hanging on for dear life because although this level is terrible, it is most certainly not as bad as the one below), and the evil advisors consumed by flame, and those whose hands were bound with ropes of poisonous snakes.

At last, having come so far, we were confronted with the Cocytus; the ultimate pit of hell. Here one finds Desire without any restraint. Here there is no recognition of moral or theological law.

"It's a funny thing," Toombs told us, "all they have to do to escape is desire it, but they never do."

"Because of pride?" I said. "Like Sisyphus."

"I suppose so," he said. "I really don't know for sure, though. Only they know, and they're not talking."

Seeing that Central Pit open itself up for us as it now did, Sarah became frantic. She began to tug on my arm, warning me back from the brink. Here, I knew, at the very center, lay the malignant worm of Satan. Here lay the Master of All Evil. When I thought of this, and of what it really meant, I too became afraid, and tried to step back.

"Where do you think you're going?" Toombs snapped, wheeling about.

"This is far enough," I said. "I've decided to go back."

"Oh, so you've decided, have you? Don't you want to see any more?"

"No, thankyou, I really don't. I've seen enough already."

"You've seen enough, isn't that a pity. But I'm sorry, there is no going back from here, whether you choose it or not."

"I was under the impression that we were immune from this place, so long as we stayed on the path."

"Who ever told you that? Oh, Dante. You seem to forget, Dante was never really here. That was all just fiction."

"I want to go back," I said stubbornly. "I want to go back."

"Of course you do," Toombs said with a smooth smile. "Everyone wants to go back once they reach this point. They never do, though. You see, it's not allowed."

Then I saw the mouth of the pit open outward like the aperture on a giant camera lens. We would be consumed. I turned to Sarah and yelled, "Run." There was a tremendous crashing noise all around us.

As we began to run, the earth crumbled away from under our feet, and we found we could not escape. Toombs' laughter was in my ears as we continued to lose ground, like ants in an ant lion's trap.

SIXTEEN

Somehow Sarah managed to escape over the edge of the pit and, reaching back to take my hand, she drew me along with her. She called my name. I came up and up and up out of the groping darkness. We had escaped the Central Pit by the skin of our teeth, as they say. I opened my eyes.

The scene that greeted me was not the expected one. Having just come over the lip of hell's final trap, I expected to once again find myself on the darkened streets of Venice. Instead, however, I was in a large subdued room into which the sunlight beyond the shutter was attempting to burst like burning magnesium.

Sarah whispered my name again. I turned my head to look at her. She was still holding my hand. I was laying in a bed with crisp white sheets. There was an I.V. pole beside me with a bag hanging on it and tubing ran down to the spot where a needle pierced the skin in the back of my hand.

"How did I get here?" I asked first thing.

"Shush now. There's plenty of time to talk later."

"What is it, have I been in an accident?" I could not remember anything after the pit. The fact frightened me.

"No," she said. "You've had a bad fever, but that's all over now."

"A fever?" I could not put what she was saying together with the night we had just been through.

"You've had a temperature of over a hundred for more than thirty hours. But your fever has broken now, and I'm sure you'll feel a lot better soon."

"Where am I?" I asked, still not certain I believed all she was saying.

"This is a doctor's clinic. The other night I pounded on doors until I found this place. You were so sick..." Tears welled up in her eyes. "I was worried about you. You're going to get better now."

I lay back in the bed for a long minute, still trying to put together what she was saying with what I knew to be true. Could it be, then, that I had been hallucinating the whole time? Could it

157

be that I had replaced reality with what I had read in the 'Inferno'? This seemed too incredible to believe.

"What's wrong?" she asked, seeing the puzzled expression on my face.

"You were with me last night? Or was it the night before?" I asked tentatively.

"Of course I was with you. Both last night, when you were so sick, and the night before, when we were lost out there in the streets."

"And did we, the night before, run into anything... unusual." I was afraid to ask. I feared I already knew the answer.

"You were very sick," she said cautiously.

"I don't want you to patronize me," I snapped. A terrible ache had wormed in behind my eyes. "Sorry," I said at once. "I'm not feeling very well yet."

"You don't need to apologize," she said. "What is it you want to know?"

"Did we run into Toombs. Did he take us... into the city of Dis."

"Into hell?" she said.

"I remember a place where the whole world was inverted. Where the steeples of the churches pointed downward. Where Satan was a revered word. Is that hell?"

"Yes, that is hell."

"Then I have been there," I said. "I thought you were there with me."

She did not say anything for a long moment. Now the shoe was on the other foot. She must have been thinking I had gone crazy. Then she said, "I don't remember having been there with you."

"We only just now escaped," I said shortly. Again I felt I should apologize, only this time I held it back. No use apologizing every minute or two.

"I don't remember," she said again, lowering her eyes.

"I'm sure of what I saw," I insisted steadfastly. "I've seen what it is like and I'm sure that I want no part of it. I think I believe the whole thing now. Angels, demons. Heaven, hell. All of it."

"Yes?" she said, looking up into my eyes again.

"You see, I've spent my whole life going this way and that, and I've never really made any choices. Well, I'm making a choice now."

Sarah nodded her understanding.

"We've descended into the depths and somehow we've come out of it again. That makes all the difference in the world to me. There's no going back now."

At that moment the doctor came into the room and, seeing me awake he said, "Good, good, good." He came over to the bedside and opened my shirt and began listening to my chest and thumping around. Then he looked into each of my eyes with his lighted scope and at last took my temperature. When he had done all this he nodded several times and said, "Good, good, good."

"How soon before we can go?" I asked Sarah, not sure how much English the good doctor might know.

"First you need sleep," the doctor said. "Then everything will be good."

"You should get some more rest," Sarah agreed.

At first I made to protest but then I realized just how tired I was. The trip into the bowels of the dark place had indeed exhausted me. I felt as if my center had been shot out with a bulls-eye target pistol. A little sleep wouldn't hurt, I reasoned.

The doctor left the room and I looked at Sarah for a long time. She smiled at me and continued to hold my hand. Her look was so tender. Her features were soft, as if I were looking at her face through a gauze veil. The warm petals of her lips were like bits of colored glass sculpted by the sea. Seeing me look at her, she bent over and kissed me.

With that kiss I floated down into sleep. I had decided. Oh yes, I had decided. In discovering her, I had also discovered myself.

Several hours passed. When I awoke Sarah was standing over near the windows. The sun must have been straight overhead, everything had a harsh noon-time look to it. The I.V. pole and tubing had been removed.

I sat up. Sarah turned to look at me. "How are you feeling?" she said.

"Much better," I said.

"I was hoping you would wake up soon. I didn't want to have to wake you."

"No?" I said.

"I explained some of what has been going on to the doctor. He has a cousin who drives a truck. His cousin is going to be leaving Venice in an hour and has agreed to take us along."

"Where is he going?"

"South," she said.

"Good, good, good," I said.

She smiled. "You must be feeling better."

"I am." I got out of bed and my head began to spin. After a moment I was able to control it.

Sarah came over to my side and helped steady me. "You shouldn't stand up so quickly."

"I'm alright," I said. "Where do we go to meet our cousin?"

"He's coming by here."

"Good, good, good."

An hour passed and then, sure enough, the cousin pulled up on the street below in his truck. We had paid the good doctor already and were now waiting impatiently to depart. Toombs was still somewhere in the city.

The man showed us on a map where he would be taking us. We would be following the Adriatic down through Ravenna and Foggia to Bari. Without any further introduction, we jumped in and the truck growled away into the traffic. Sarah was in the middle and I was on the window side. I could feel her leg warm against mine.

We came upon Ravenna, an old city that looked oddly like a cardboard cutout from a distance, late in the afternoon. In the days of the Romans, Ravenna had been a town set in a lagoon, very much like Venice. Now it was on dry ground.

From there we continued south. The sun set and after it was completely dark, it was perhaps ten o'clock by then, our driver, the cousin, began to show signs of eye strain. He made exaggerated gestures with his hands to prove that he was, indeed, very tired. After another half hour he pulled the truck into a stop along the road. There, apologetically, he handed us each a blanket and gestured that we could all sleep under the truck, which was what he was going to do.

I looked at Sarah and could see that she had no objections. She was a good sport, that woman.

Without any further discussion, we laid our blankets out on the rough ground under the truck and rolled up in them. We could hear the sea nearby in the dark. Because I was still not completely recuperated, I fell asleep almost at once.

During the night I had the dream again. The black knight attacked me and I warded off his charge with my staff. Then the white knight turned away, and left me alone. Later, when my subconscious had almost forgotten that dream, I was having another. This time my father was sitting at the kitchen table talking to me. "Do you remember those two knights?" he asked me.

I nodded my assent, though surprised that he knew anything at all about the dream. I had never told him about it.

"The white knight was me."

I woke up. Sarah and the driver were still sleeping but already the sun was cheering up the eastern horizon, out over the calm sea. The sound of the waves on the shore settled me.

My father had hanged himself the year before. His death scared me more than anything else that has ever happened to me. In the years that I had known him, he was the strongest man in the world. He could build things, and fight, and work and swear and drink and smoke and holler and bull down any obstacle in his path. People loved him or they hated him. There was never any middle ground. If he loved you, there wasn't a thing in the world he wouldn't do for you. But if he hated you (the word dislike was not, I don't believe, in his vocabulary), he was the worst enemy you ever had in this world.

He was a man of vision who could actually make things work. Some of the schemes he tried came down in a Zorba-like splendiferous crash, but many things he tried turned out well. He could laugh, (I will remember that wonderful laugh all my days), and he could cry. In spite of his tough exterior, he was in touch with the world. He was sensitive to the feelings of others.

Then, at some point in his life, the world began to eat away at him little by little. He lost his first finger and part of his thumb in an accident at work. All of his kids moved away. He gave up the home he had built with his own two hands and began to roam around, looking for some other place. But no place was ever quite as good again. He became depressed, and began to take medications to lift his spirits. He was in and out of the hospital.

He wrote me long, lonesome letters which I did not know how to respond to.

He hanged himself, I think, to spare himself and us, and the world, any more pain. (The white knight rode off and left us to muddle through our own miserable little lives).

I remember thinking, when it happened, that now none of us have a chance in this world. If depression and madness and shame could so easily destroy a man as great as he, then the rest of us are helpless indeed. That is what scared me most. That there was no hope.

Now, with Sarah, I had begun to hope again. Every kiss from her lips pulled me further up out of myself. She had torn the corner off my life, and the sweet air was rushing into the vacuum that had formed there. I knew, when I looked at her, that I could go on.

When Sarah woke up, I went over to her and pulled her to me without a word and kissed her. She did not question anything but hugged me and as our lips parted she lay her head against my chest. After a time she said, "I like to hear your heart beating."

"May it beat a thousand years for your enjoyment," I said.

She looked up into my eyes and smiled. "I know that you love me," she said.

"Yes," I said. "And do you love me?"

"You know that I do. I will love you for a thousand years, and then we'll just be getting warmed up."

Once our driver the cousin had gotten himself awake, we headed on down the road. In Foggia he pulled into the Piazza Cavour and pointed on the map that he was going on to Bari.

"I told the doctor that we were going to Naples," Sarah told me. "I guess this is where we get off for Naples."

"One place is as good as another," I said, "in our situation."

"That's true, but you see we could get trapped down here in the boot of Italy." She pointed at the map. "We might never get out."

"I see what you mean. You're one smart lady." I nodded my appreciation. "I guess we'd better go on over to Naples."

Speaking with his hands and his feet, (I don't know where I ever heard that expression, but it has always stayed with me), the cousin told us he might find a ride for us, going west towards Naples. He left the cab of the truck, and after a few moments he returned. He had, indeed, found us a ride.

We thanked the cousin very much for all his help and transferred ourselves over to the beer truck that was to take us across the ankle of Italy. Our driver was a boisterous sort, (unlike the cousin, who had been quiet). He pointed at us with his stodgy forefinger and said, "Napoli?" I nodded. Then he pointed to himself and said, "Napoli."

Taking up the game I pointed to him and said, "You, Napoli." Then I pointed to myself and said, "Me, Napoli."

The man laughed and nodded his whole-hearted encouragement. He went at everything, in fact, whole-heartedly. He reminded me of my father.

The morning had become hot and arid. As we headed out of town, the air felt good blowing in on us from the window. Once we hit the open road, the beer-truck driver pulled out a narrow paper sack that was filled with hard bread rolls. He offered them over to us with a great beaming smile on his face. We tore into them gratefully, not having had anything to eat since the previous afternoon. When we had finished, he passed over a bottle of red wine. "No birra," he said, making a face. He pointed toward the back of the truck and twisted up his features once again. "Birra."

"I don't think he likes beer," I said. I hoisted the bottle of wine and took a drink, then handed it to Sarah. She took a drink and made a face in spite of herself. The driver laughed. "Birra," he said, and shook his head.

We continued on toward Naples, three people thrown together by who knows what fates.

Before we got into the city, we came upon a square where a group of men and boys were carrying banners and clubs and all were shouting, "Vota Socialista".

"Communisti," said the driver in a suddenly cautious tone.

There were a few policemen around, with pistols drawn.

"Communisti," the driver said again. He motioned us to get down in our seats. We obliged him. We passed through the area without incident and further on, down near the bay, he dropped us off.

We waved and thanked him and he waved and then said, "Birra," and made his face again. We all laughed and then he pulled away and was gone around the next corner.

The day had lost some of its luster now as the sun headed for the western ocean. The dazzle of light off the waves was nearly blinding, but the heat had abated. We walked along in silence for some time, holding hands, not knowing where we were going. We didn't care, really. Sooner or later we would find a hotel. Then the entire rest of our life would begin.

As we walked, a thousand conventional words came into my head. Where could I start a conversation with such weightless fluff? We were already beyond the point of making light or worse, polite, conversation. But we had not yet reached the intimacy one must reach to set a new tone to things. Already we had exhausted ten thousand imaginings about each other. What we had imagined of each other coated the distance between us with honey.

Sarah broke the silence at last by saying, "You were up early this morning."

"A dream woke me up."

"A pleasant one, I hope."

"It wasn't a nightmare, if that's what you mean. But it wasn't pleasant, either."

"Was it about me?"

"No," I said. To broach that subject, I would have to break through that last veil of intimacy, I realized. At first I did not know if I wanted to do that. Sarah would make a great lover, I was convinced, but could she be more than that? Would not her madness stand between us at every turn. And what of my own madness. With my visit to the underworld, I felt terribly unsteady myself. How could I, then, explain about the dream and about my father and all the rest of it?

"You don't have to tell me," she said, pouting so as to salve her injured feelings.

"I'll tell you," I said, making up my mind at only that very moment. "It was a dream about my father. He was a white knight. He left me."

"He left you?"

"He killed himself. Weren't you there?" This last was an unkind addition I could not resist.

"I don't know where I've been," she said, taking the barb without comment. "You're in pain because you have lost your father. But I have lost my father too. I've lost heaven and everyone I've ever known. Whether because of madness, as you suggest, or because of the wiles of Morton Toombs, I don't know. What's more, it doesn't really make any difference. Loss is painful, no matter what causes it."

"I guess I hadn't thought of it that way."

"Did you love your father?"

"Yes, very much. My father taught me how to live. But then he forgot how to live himself. What was I supposed to do?" Tears welled up in my eyes. "What was I supposed to do?"

"There wasn't anything you could have done," she said softly. "He's not a ghost, you know. He's a white knight. You must remember him kindly."

"But will he ever rest in peace? Tell me that, if you can."

"He will rest in peace, if you let him."

"I miss the days when he was strong, and I was weak."

"You will see him again," she assured me. "And when you do, he'll be the strong one. He'll lead the way."

We walked along several steps again quietly. Then Sarah said, "Thankyou for telling me about your father."

All of the barriers between us were down now. We were inextricably bound together. There was only one thing that could make us closer than we were now. The time had come.

First, however, we had to eat. We were both famished, and growing shaky from our fatigue and lack of food. We found a little restaurant on the Piazza Trieste and there we had spaghetti and steak and Chianti mixed with mineral water. From time to time we let our hands touch across the table and we gazed into each others eyes. Each time I looked at her I saw a different person or, perhaps to be more exact, a different facet of the same person. Her face was a hologram into which I could read so many shapes and textures, but which were really all only a new play of light and shadow.

"Is this a dream?" I asked her. "Are you just an illusion, a figment of my imagination?"

"Why do you ask that?" she said, drawing back a little, to take a better look at me.

"I've been having a feeling of unreality ever since I left home. No, that's not true. Things seemed unreal even before that. But before I left, at least, I thought I could control my life. Now I'm not certain of anything. Do you know what I mean? I told you I've made my choice, only, saying and doing are two different things. It's just not that simple. I'm just struggling to find my way every single day."

"I know exactly what you mean," she said, nodding emphatically. "We've been pulled out of our normal everyday lives, and we don't know for what purpose. That's the way I feel, anyway."

"The trouble is, I don't feel I belong here. I don't know where I belong. Maybe I belong in some other time. My father said he was born a hundred years too late. That's what killed him, I think. Maybe I was born too early, or too late. A person born out of his own time has no one to confide in."

"It would be easier if we had been given some instructions, wouldn't it."

"Exactly. If I knew what it was all about, I wouldn't feel nearly so afraid."

"Maybe it's just about us," she said. "Maybe it's about you and me, meeting and falling in love."

"Is that enough? Is that enough in God's great plan. Shouldn't there be more?"

"There's always more. But for right now, yes, it is enough."

"That's comforting to hear," I said, "if only it's true."

"We can't go back," she said. "There's only one way for us."

I took her hand up and kissed it. It was soft against my lips.

"I have lost my heaven and you have lost your home," she said. "Now there is only us."

SEVENTEEN

I was still reeling from the many various turns the events of my life had taken in the past weeks. The feelings of unreality or, rather, of uncertainty about reality, continued to plague me even as time slowed between us. In short order I had learned to trust nothing that my senses told me, but to base my actions on a kind of intuitive 'feeling' that comes from within, not from without. Never before in my life, (except perhaps in those days when I had written stories), had I experienced this other sense of things. My insistence upon clinging to the past had left me struggling to find my way. Now, however, I felt myself ready to step out into the vast unknown.

It is here, where the unknown begins, that the worlds of gods and men overlap. No wonder we fear it. In this place all of the rules we have learned for our life have been suspended. If we are to enter through this portal, we must become more like gods than men. We must lay aside what we know of our world, and willingly accept the greater Way that lies open to us.

Love can take us to this place. Not that physical groping between two sweating bodies in a tameless night bed that some have come to see as love. (An entire industry has grown up around giving men and women glimpses of 'perfect' beauty; faces and bodies so perfect that even the models themselves could never hope to live up to them without computer and photo enhancements). No, the pleasures of the flesh are momentary. Love is eternal.

But are not love and madness close cousins? I wondered. Are not ecstatic religious visions and fanaticism two edges of the same sword? By falling in love, was I not also opening myself up to the possibility of delirious insanity. By embracing that which was mystical and mysterious, was I not also opening the Pandora's box of paganism? These are the questions that caused my fear that evening.

Quite unexpectedly, then, I had come to the true turning point of my life. From here I must either go forward toward possibility, or return back up the way I had come, to certainty. (The price one pays for wisdom is uncertainty, I have since discovered, and the price one pays for certitude is narrowness). Now that I had reached this place, I found myself completely unprepared to make the decision.

On the one hand, I feared what lay ahead. As I have said before, insanity has been the one overwhelming nemesis in my life. By letting go my past, which had served for so long as an anchor, as a tap root, would I not also be letting go of my grip on reality altogether. The past weeks had proven already that I was capable of much insanity. Somewhere along the way my grandmother and grandfather and father all had let go, or had been torn from, that center structure which keeps us securely in our world of focus. Perhaps all of them had been facing a dilemma similar to the one I now faced. Perhaps they had been forced to make this choice, just as I now must, and had chosen the wrong one. Then, having gone the wrong way, had wound down into inevitable insanity, without a single hope of ever getting back.

On the other hand, (why must there always be another hand?), I could return to the life I had been leading; that long, dull, lonely existence in which I smothered a little more each day, and then I could still go insane. That would be the final insult, would it not? To have given up what lay ahead out of fear, and then to have become afflicted by the very malady you had feared in the first place. How can one ever decide anything, I wondered.

Looking across the table at Sarah now, however, I knew that the deed was done already. I had fallen in love with her. I would go, and in fact had gone to hell and back for her. I would face the many and varied nameless torments of madness to be near her. I would break all of the rules of gods and men to make love with her. The life I had been living without her seemed old and flat and stale now that her light shined back upon it. There could be no future for me that did not also include her.

Her sculpted face of a Greek goddess glowed warmly in the evening light coming in by the windows. (I was feeling particularly poetic at that moment). Her honey colored hair caught the glow and held it fast. Her left hand was soft in mine as we again picked up our glasses and with an unspoken toast, drank to us, and to our future. We looked longingly into each other's eyes.

"What have you been thinking?" she asked me, setting her glass back down on the table.

"I've been thinking about you. About us," I corrected.

"What about us?"

"Where do we go from here? That's what I've been wondering."

"Where do you want us to go from here?" She made a quizzical look with her eyebrows.

"I don't know, I'm so in love with you. I don't know how it happened."

"I'm in love with you too," she said. "So I guess we'd better do the things that lovers do."

"Yes?" The beating of my heart stepped up.

She had a way of putting things so simply. I could not understand how she could capture with ease the very matters I struggled with so intently. At times like these she seemed, well, angelic.

"It's getting dark," she said. "We really should go and find a room."

I glanced at the windows. The last rays of the sun had vanished over the horizon, leaving a bright smudge of orange on the sunset. Without another word I stood up, paid the bill, and then led the way outside.

Once we were out on the sidewalk our hands touched and we walked along, holding hands, with our shoulders snug together. At one point I bent over and kissed her.

"We do love each other, don't we?" she said.

"Yes, we do."

"It's not just some silly little infatuation, is it?"

"No, it's not. We've been together long enough now to know our feelings."

"That's true," she nodded. "We've known each other for all eternity."

I never became used to her saying things like that. Her words always gave me a little shock. I guess this was because I wanted to forget about her problem - that of believing herself to be an angel. If she could simply have set that aside, I would not have been nearly so unsure of myself. Just because I had somehow fallen in love with her, though, did not mean that I did not have my reservations.

Sarah seemed perfectly content to continue along as she was - not knowing who she was or where she had come from. This, to me, was the most astonishing part of the whole affair. If I had been in her place, I'm quite sure I would have launched an all-out effort at once to discover this vital information. It was beyond me how she could continue to function the way she had, without a clue about her past. What is more, I suspected that at any time this lack was going to hunt her down from behind, and claim her. Still, there seemed to be nothing I could do to help her in this regard.

There was always that shadow between us, and the shadow of Morton Toombs. No matter how close we might become, I could never be sure that her past would not loom up before us at any moment, like some god-awful dragon, with overwhelming reasons to split us apart. Are we not all in a way a consequence of our past?

(Do the events of our lives, one wonders, express the sum of our personal feelings. Do the events of history express the total of our collective desires?)

At any moment, too, Toombs could rear his ugly head with his cold instincts of a trained assassin, and cut short our joy, not to mention our lives. His presence everywhere around us put a certain edge on our everyday affairs. The dark tides of his evil existence were always there, just under the surface.

Despite the vacation air of the city, as we walked along, we felt as if we were secret co-conspirators, living lives that were separate somehow from the other people around us, and thus special. We were intriguing in the city, and this gave a certain luster to everything.

We were in love. The thought bubbled up into my chest like a surprising red balloon. I wanted to shout it out so that everyone would know. "We are in love!" "We are in love." "We are in love!"

So, that is why every clandestine activity is so demanding. The one involved in such activity feels special, and thus is inclined to want everyone else to know. We would have to make every effort to keep our secrets to ourselves.

Abruptly I stopped and turned quickly to scan the streets and doorways around us. A man who had been walking behind us scowled and veered to miss running into us. A few steps later he muttered something unintelligible under his breath.

"What is it?" Sarah asked, looking around fearfully.

"Nothing," I said. "I was just checking for Toombs."

"Oh," she said. Her face fell glumly. It was clear that she had managed, at least for the time being, to put him out of her mind. "Do we have to think about him every minute?"

"I don't see him," I said in a soothing tone. "Sorry. I guess I need to relax."

"No, you're right. Of course you are. We should never let our guard down."

Along the way we stopped in at a little shop to buy some toiletry items. Then we came to a hotel, the Sogno, and there we inquired about a room. Finding everything to our liking, we paid for the room and went upstairs at once and settled in.

"I just love these European hotels," Sarah said in an affected tone. "They're much nicer than the ones over in the States, don't you think?"

"They're grand," I said.

"If it wasn't for... oh, you know, everything, I'd be having a perfectly wonderful time."

"Yes?"

"Oh, I don't mean that I'm not having a good time."

I went over to her and kissed her on the lips. We held each other's lips so long that we nearly collapsed into a heap right there on the floor. Finally we parted and I whispered, "We don't need to be afraid. We love each other."

"I'm not afraid," she said.

"Well I am, a little. But I don't know why."

"It's a big change," she said, looking up into my face.

"That's it," I admitted. "I've always been afraid of change."

"Aren't we all," she said. (It was at moments like this that she seemed the most human).

"I'll tell you what," I said, finally making up my mind, "why don't you let me go in and take a bath. Then, when I get out, you can have one."

"Aren't you afraid I'll get away from you again?"

"I'll just track you down like last time," I said with a smile. "Why don't you save us both a lot of trouble and stay here."

"I'll wait for you, I promise."

While I was in the bath I listened carefully to assure myself that she was not attempting another escape. I could hear her humming a little tune I had never heard before, so keeping track of her was not difficult. All the while my mind was conjugating various patterns of love in wonderful combinations. My imaginings were getting the better of me. My body thrilled at the very thought of her. Breathlessly I washed and then cleared out of the bath as fast as I could.

When I had finished cleaning the tub, I wrapped the towel around myself and went into the other room. Sarah turned back from the window to look at me.

"Why don't you lay there on the bed while I have my bath," she said.

"Aren't you afraid I'll go to sleep?" I asked.

She laughed. "I'll wake you up as soon as I'm done."

Then she went into the bathroom and I lay on top of the bed and let the springy breeze from the window blow over me. My mind was floating, waiting for her.

For a time I could hear her splashing around in there and then all grew quiet. Finally she interrupted my thoughts by calling, "Could you come and help me?"

I came up out of myself all at once, with a start. I wondered if I had been dozing.

"I'll be right there."

The darkness had grown deeper. I got off the bed and went into the bathroom. She was still laying in the tub. A layer of soap bubbles on top of the water obscured my view of her.

"What is it you wanted?" I asked.

With a wincing grin she raised up from the bath a bit and turned to show me the back of her right shoulder. There I saw a surprising discolored bruise. "I'm a might stiff back here," she said.

"What. How did this happen? Is this from that fight the other day? Did Toombs cause this?" I stepped up to take a closer look.

"He hit me when I tried to get away."

I felt anger rise up like bile in the back of my throat. My face flushed red. "I'll kill that son-of-a..."

"It's not that," Sarah said quickly. "We'd be better off if we never saw him again. I don't want you fighting him over me."

"But... what then?"

"I want to shave my legs." She lifted one out of the water to show me. It was a beautiful leg. "Only, my back is so painful, I don't know if I can."

"So you want me to help you..." I said the words before I had considered their full meaning.

"Have you ever done that before?"

"Never," I assured her.

"Do you mind?" She looked up into my face.

My breathing became so short I began to feel light-headed. "I'll do it," I said. A sense of recklessness came over me.

She pointed at the razor and the can of shaving cream sitting on the ledge of the tub. "Are you sure it won't be too much trouble? I don't want to be any trouble to you."

"It's no trouble," I said quickly. My stomach was clenched tight. I wondered what I was so nervous about. "Aren't you afraid I'll cut you?"

"I know you'll be gentle," she said.

My heart beat the faster. I picked up the razor and after inspecting its fine cutting edge, swished it in the water. Then I set it aside and picked up the can of shaving cream. This I shook vigorously for some seconds. (I was stalling for time, as you might have guessed). At last I pressed a dab out into my hand, just as if I were getting ready to shave my own face.

Again Sarah drew her leg out of the water and placed it, provocatively, on the rim of the tub. I caught my breath and marveled at the long expanse of her leg from her ankle to her thigh. The rest of her was still hidden in the water.

My hand positively shook as I reached down to smooth the shaving cream up and down her calf. When I picked up the razor, we both could see how unsteady I was.

"Are you sure you're up to this?" she asked in a teasing tone.

I swallowed deep and then said, "I'll do my best."

She closed her eyes in mock terror. This gave me another long moment to look her over. As I knelt there in my towel, I looked again at her long right leg, and at her left knee where it poked out of the water without a care in the world. And then at her upper breasts, and her rounded shoulders and long neck. Her eyes were closed, as I have said, and her lips were parted slightly. The lower part of her hair was wet and clung here and there against the sides of her face and around her ears. Then she opened her eyes abruptly and caught me staring. "Aren't you going to do it?" she asked. "I trust you." There was nothing coy in her voice now. We both knew where all of this was headed. Trouble was, I didn't know how long I could last.

"I was just going to," I said defensively. I bent seriously to the task.

Sarah giggled and I pulled back as if scalded. "I didn't mean to interrupt," she said, and giggled again. "You have such an intent look on your face, that's all."

"I want to do it right," I said.

"You'll do just fine."

Again I bent over her leg. At first the razor seemed to rasp against the stubble, and I was afraid to give it any pressure. I knew how to gauge the right amount of pressure to use on my own face, of course, but I was quite sure that her legs were much softer. "I'm not hurting you, am I?"

"No," she said, "but you'll have to press harder than that if you want to get them smooth."

In spite of my fears, I pressed harder. At any moment I feared she would scream and that all my precautions would have been in vain. Every so often I glanced up at her face, to see if I was causing her any pain. Each time I looked, however, she only smiled.

"How am I doing?" I asked, still fearing the worst.

"You're doing just fine. Don't worry about a thing."

When it came time to begin on her left leg, she leaned back even further in the water and exposed more of her leg to my view. I didn't know if my heart could stand it. That sounds funny, I'm sure, but I'm very serious. This short period of delay was almost more than I could bear. I truly believed that I might faint at any moment.

"I do love you," she sighed.

I glanced up at her again to find her head lolling back on the rear of the tub, and her eyes closed. By the sound of her voice she seemed ready to release herself against the touch of my hand on her leg. I could feel her excitement in myself.

In order to scrape off the last bit of shaving cream near her ankle, I was forced to take her entire foot in my hand. As I did so she groaned ever so slightly, and eased even further back in the water. When I looked at her face I caught her in the act of licking her lips.

Once I had finished with the razor I set it aside, but kept her foot firmly in my hand. Cautiously at first, I brushed over the top of it with my fingers. I followed its curve down to the tops of her toes and then I reversed my motion, stroking back along the underside of her arch. Without conscious effort she drew her toes up and allowed me full access to the bottom of her foot.

Hungrily, I now put my lips to her arch. She groaned yet again, though slightly louder this time, and her whole leg quivered. My mouth slipped along the soft valley of the side of her foot until I was able to kiss the inside of her ankle. She caught her breath and then I saw her lick her lips again. The quick pink tip of her tongue was startling and sensuous at once.

At that moment, (I thought I had done something wrong), she pulled her foot away. But then the next moment she was reaching out her arms to me. I met her arms and her waiting lips.

"I can't wait," I said in a whisper, when my lips at last escaped hers. "I can't wait another minute."

"I know," she said. "I can't either."

I took her towel up from the floor as she stood, and began helping her dry herself. She stepped out of the tub and finished drying her legs, wiping away the last of the shaving cream I had left there. I pulled her to me again and she reached down to my side and unfastened the knot I had made in my towel.

Holding her body against mine, I could not help but notice a warmth flow through me that I had never felt before. At each place our skin touched together, a kind of penetrating heat seeped into me. Our bodies were on fire. The smell of her skin and hair was sweet lilac. I could feel the tip of her tongue against mine.

We went into the other room and lay down on the bed and pressed against one another so hard we thought we might break into pieces. There was no turning back now, no matter what. The demands of our desires had taken us over. We had but a single purpose between us.

Her meekness had completely vanished now. Her whole body became an extension of her inescapable desire. Her breath was in my ear, urging me on. We seemed to be breathing for each other now. We had become completely a part of one another.

At a certain moment I became detached from myself. Somewhere in my head I heard the sound of wings. I drew up and up and up out of my body. I looked around in surprise. I was no longer who I had been.

EIGHTEEN

How can I describe for you, dear reader, the feelings that come from the union of a man and an angel? (At that moment I was prepared to believe anything. Truly, she was of heaven). It was as if I had experienced a sudden shift in my way of seeing, and had at last discovered eternity. It was something vast and magnificent and mysterious and inscrutable.

Our two tiny souls had somehow found each other in the vastness of all time and of all space to create between us this one moment of tender, satiated happiness. What had happened before to lead us to this place was rendered insignificant. Whatever might happen from now on would be inconsequential. The only thing that mattered now, in this instant of cosmic bonding, was the inevitability of our love for one another.

In spite of all I thought I knew about love, it came as a painful realization. I truly did love her. All was transformed. My life would never be the same again. To relieve that sudden distress in the center of my being I said, in a desperate way, "I'll love you forever and then forever again."

She did not say anything as she held me to her breast, but I felt her begin to sob quietly, and I supposed great silent tears were flowing down her face.

I wanted to apologize for anything I had said or done wrong, but could not think of the words to use. I remember experiencing at that moment an emotion I cannot even now fully describe. It was a vague feeling of emptiness and longing, of something irrevocably lost, but also, strangely, of peace and wholeness. I had never felt so full in my life. (This sounds oxymoronic, I know, but it is as near as my pitiful crabby little scribblings will ever come to explaining it). It was, in short, the whole life-death, heaven-hell, man-woman, light-darkness, interconnectedness-of-things feeling hitting me all at once.

Now that I had reached this unexpected stage of my development, I tried to cast back in my mind to remember precisely how I had come to be here. Where before everything had seemed to proceed along in fits and starts, from this vantage it all appeared seamless, as if it had been intended this way all along. This sudden connection with the eternal had caused me to lose my place in history. The events of my life had led me forward without my permission to this moment, and now I wondered why I had ever questioned the course of my wanderings at all. (So perfect was the outcome).

All of those inexhaustible hopes and awesome moments of magic and curious gifts and tiny transforations and strange happenings and flashes of fear and horror had been like dreams and nightmares. They had grown out of proportion and had branched off and multiplied until they had become unrecognizable from the originals, and still they had continued unabated. They had led me through stretches of uncertain geography and curious adventures and into misfortunes and absurdities. They had led me through difficulties and trials and enchantments and into a new conscious-ness. When a man meets heaven, I at last understood, he begins to see things differently from then on.

Everything else seemed like a dream encompassed within a dream wrapped within another dream. Where does one leave off and the next begin? (Please bear with me, fellow reader, as this line of thought continues to develop). I felt that I had become a spectator of my own life. I relate these things now as if they have happened to another. I did not know what was real and what was part of the magic of that single eternal moment.

There was one thing I did know for certain, however. I knew that I was tired of living my life alone. I was tired of fumbling along in my ignorance. (I had spent the coin of my youth here frivolously and there fearfully, and I had nothing to show for it). It was only then, when I found Sarah, that I knew what I had wanted all along. It was only then that I knew how lonely I had been.

As I lay there, I continued trying to understand precisely what it was I was feeling. But the more I concentrated upon it, and the more I determined to identify it, the farther away it flew. I had discovered a hidden treasure, but was still unsure of its true nature and value.

Coming out into the light from the shadows of my life-long fears now, I hungered for her smile. She had stopped crying, and lay quietly stroking the hair on the back of my head with her fingers. At last I ventured a look up into her face. Light from the other room fell on her, and I noticed her sad expression. Her look was grave, as if somehow suspecting what lay ahead for us. But, I wonder now, how could that have been?

"Is it wrong for us to be in love?" I asked.

She shifted her gaze to look into my eyes. "It isn't wrong," she said.

"What is it then? What is wrong?"

Her eyes brimmed with tears again. There was some terrible pain hidden deep within her that she seemed unable to release.

"I've told you that I'll love you forever..."

"It's not that," she said, smiling wanly.

"Whatever it is, I know I can help make it better. Why don't you give me a chance?"

She shook her head slightly and then tried to smile again. I could not tell what terrible mood possessed her.

During the night I dreamed that I saw Sarah standing over near the windows. She was glowing a soft white color and when she turned to look at me I could see her great huge wings. Without a word of explanation to me, she stretched out those wings and began to slowly flap them back and forth as a butterfly might, drying in the sun. On her face was a look of extreme ecstasy.

I got up from the bed and went over to her. "You 'are' an angel," I marveled. I reached out for her.

"Don't touch me now," she cautioned. "Soon I will be in heaven again."

When I woke up, the dream seemed as if it had been real. I could not tell whether I had been awake or asleep. But Sarah was still in the bed beside me.

I lay there feeling confused for a long moment.

Why had the dream seemed so real? What did it mean? And also, I had the vague feeling that I had been hearing a loud noise in my sleep. That something besides only my dream had awakened me. I looked at my watch. It was only three a.m.

At last I settled back and dozed again, I don't know for how long. It was probably only a minute or two before I was jerked up out of my sleep again by a loud noise. For a moment I thought I was in the army and someone was firing howitzers in the distance.

"What was that?" Sarah bolted up from her sleep with a start.

In a way, I was glad she had heard it too. I had suspected I was dreaming again.

"It was a noise," I said, "out in the hallway."

We heard it again. It was an abrupt, flat, slamming sound. This was followed by the sound of startled voices, and then by a scream. I scrambled out of the bed and, pulling one of the blankets around my nakedness, went to the door. I opened it a crack and peered out into the hall.

There was more shouting and another scream. I could not yet see what was going on. The slamming sound echoed up the hall again. I leaned further out.

It was Toombs. Someone - an Italian man, tried to grab his arm. Toombs punched him in the face with his elbow and the Italian flew back against the wall in animated suddenness. A woman sobbed and rushed over to the man.

Toombs came down to the next door, about five up from our own, reared back and knocked it down with a single sure kick. There were more shouts of surprise and fear, and further screams and general mayhem followed. People were running up and down the halls. Someone was yelling down the stairs, apparently hoping for help from security.

Unconcerned by all this, Toombs came down to the next door and readied himself to repeat the actions.

Sarah was beside me now. "It's him," she said in a strained whisper. "I knew it was him."

"We'd better get out of here."

"How can we?"

"Get some clothes on. Quick." I began pulling my pants on.

There was another whooshing crash. That door had gone. He was searching for us, that much was clear. He'd keep kicking in doors until he found us.

We did not wait to get completely dressed. Instead, we went again to the door, half dressed, and waited. When the big man had concentrated all his attention on that next door, we sneaked out into the hall and headed up the way, away from him, and found the stairway on the far end of the building. He had not seen us.

As we went down the stairs, we hurriedly pulled on the rest of our clothes, and by the time we reached the lobby, we looked halfway presentable again.

There, men and women were streaming down the main stairway, and were pouring out of the lift, fleeing the maniac on the floor above. At the same time, uniformed police and the manager in his suit, and several men in hotel uniforms, were attempting to make their way up the stairs. They were going to try to apprehend the man we knew to be invincible.

In all the commotion, we slipped out through the main entrance and hailed a taxi. The driver seemed sleepy and shrugged nonchalantly when we told him to hurry us over to the train station. Surely, he must have been thinking, no one needed be in such a hurry so early in the morning. Still, he made good time driving up the Corso Umberto I to the Piazza Garibaldi and the Stazione Centrale.

We were in luck, too. The next Rapido headed for Rome via Cassino was leaving in five minutes. We had just enough time to purchase our tickets and to get out to the track. No sooner had we settled into our seats than the train bumped and lurched and then pulled away.

"That was close," I said, heaving a sigh of relief. "Too close."

"He is always right behind us," Sarah said, leaning back and closing her eyes. "I believe he will pursue us through all eternity."

"I'll have to confront him sooner or later," I said. "We can't run forever."

"It won't do you any good to confront him until you're strong enough to beat him. Otherwise you will only die."

"I don't know if I'll ever be that strong," I admitted. "He threw me around like a rag doll last time."

"That's the wrong kind of strong. Of course you can't beat him with only your body. You must be stronger within yourself. You must know what to do."

"When will I ever be that strong? How will I know when I have that kind of strength?"

"You will know you're that strong when you know what to do. Until then, we have to run."

"What about you? Will you never be that strong?"

"Not as long as I'm here on this earth. As long as I am here, he will have power over me. That is why I must depend on you."

"And if I fail?"

"Then we both fail. We are together, you know, for all eternity."

"Yes," I said quietly, "I know."

We arrived at the Stazione Termini in Rome, without further incident, less than two hours later. It was then five fifteen in the morning, and the sun was just coming up over the horizon.

Near the station I was able to rent a car, a small Ford, using the papers I had been given at the police station in Verona in place of a passport. "It is possible in Italy," the woman told us, "to drive a car with only your United States driver's license."

From the Via Marsala, where we rented the car, we crossed over to the Via Cavour and then up to the Via del Quirinale, passing between the two hills, the Quirinal and the Viminal, and then we made our way over to the Piazza Venezia at the head of the Via del Corso. Driving up the Corso we passed the Pantheon, on the left, and the Via Condotti and the Spanish Steps, on the right. We passed through the Piazza del Popolo and then drove up the Via Flaminia until we were able to get onto the Autostrada.

"That has to have been the shortest tour of Rome ever made," Sarah commented, once we had gotten out on the highway.

"I'm not much in the mood for sightseeing," I said seriously.

She laughed shortly. "No, of course not."

The morning was clear and dry and there was surprisingly little traffic on the Autostrada del Sole (A-1) that led north toward Florence. It felt good to be driving a car again, after having been at the mercy of so many other various modes of transportation in the past weeks. With the steering wheel in my hands, it seemed as if I controlled my own destiny again at last. Now we could evade Toombs indefinitely. Or so I thought.

Morton Toombs remained a mystery to me then. I still could not understand how he got from place to place so quickly, and without seeming to use any normal means of transportation. We had seen him on the train once, when he followed us there, but otherwise he seemed simply to materialize out of thin air. (Even then, on the train, his sudden appearance had been like a magician's). And he always found us with surprising ease, no matter how far we had run, or in which direction. It was uncanny, when I thought of it.

"How do you suppose Toombs knows so much about us?" I asked Sarah, continuing my thoughts out loud.

"He knows our very souls," she said gravely.

We stopped once, in the medieval fortress town of Orvieto, where we ate a light breakfast at a coffee bar. Then we got back out on the road and arrived in Florence by mid-morning.

Once we arrived in the city, we parked the car and walked for the better part of an hour to stretch our legs. We began in the Piazza del Duomo with its Cathedral of Santa Maria del Fiore and then proceeded up the Via Cerrentani and the Via Conti to the Church of San Lorenzo. (Please forgive me these mini travelogs. I am telling them as much to myself as to you, my reader, to keep the events straight in my own mind). From there we went over to the Church of Santa Maria Novella and then down the Via de Fossi to the Piazza Goldoni and over the Arno River on the Ponte alla Carraia.

For a time we followed the Arno along the Lungarno Torrigiani to the Ponte Vecchio - (the old bridge). Here we recrossed the Arno, looking in on the shops of the goldsmiths and jewelers along the bridge, and followed the Via Por Santa Maria to the open-air loggia called the Mercato Nuovo with its many souvenir stands and its Porcellino fountain.

There was something to see in every direction, but we had no time to see it. We stopped to eat lunch just after noon, since we did not know when we would eat again. We went down some steps into a buca restaurant (literally - a 'hole' restaurant), which was located in a cellar below the sidewalk. We ordered the buglione, a meat and vegetable stew, with salad and bread, and a bottle of wine.

"With any luck, we'll be out of Italy this afternoon," I told Sarah.

Again that sad look came into her eyes, as if she knew very well what was going to happen to us, and could do nothing to prevent any of it.

We finished our meal in silence and when we had gone back out into the bright sunny day, I spotted Toombs. He was walking in the market area we had just left and was showing a photograph to anyone he chanced to meet. I pointed him out to Sarah and said, "That must be a picture of us. Where could he have gotten our picture?"

She shook her head, she did not know, and then grabbed my arm and coaxed me up the Via de Calzaiuoli which led us, after a few minutes, back up to the Campanile (the Bell Tower) on the Piazza del Duomo.

It took us several minutes of frantic searching to find the place we had parked the car, and then we were on our way again. "How does he find us so easily?" I wondered aloud.

Sarah did not answer.

I made several false turnings before I was able to find my way back out onto the highway that would take us through Lucca and La Spezia to Genoa. Pushing hard, we made Genoa in little over two hours.

"He's nearby," Sarah said mysteriously as we pulled off the Autostrada. "I can feel him."

"How can he be anywhere nearby?" I asked reasonably. "We've just driven two hours as fast as we could go. No way could he have known where we'd be headed. There's no way he could have gotten here ahead of us."

"You still don't know him," Sarah said with a sigh.

"You're just letting your fears get the better of you. He's a maniac, yes. He's a psychopath. He has great powers because he is crazy. His adrenalin probably pumps all the time. But he isn't supernatural. He can't just fly through the air."

"You must help me," Sarah said.

I glanced at her. Her knuckles were white where her hand was clutching the top of the dash.

"Relax," I said quietly. "I'll do everything I can to help you."

"You have to do more than you can do."

"What does that mean?" I said. We were coming down into the city now.

"You have to believe."

I nearly laughed, but then reigned myself in. The only thing I believed then was that we had to escape this madman, Toombs, once and for all. (How was it, I wondered, that madness had followed me around like this, all my life. Are some people destined, or perhaps genetically chosen, to flee that malady every moment they spend on this earth? It is like fleeing a part of yourself).

To avoid the labyrinthian streets of the city, we followed the Nuova Metroplitana Leggera along the port. There, just across from the Ponte Spinola on the Piazza Caricamento, stood Morton

Toombs. I spotted him the very moment he threw a large paving stone at the car. It struck the door on Sarah's side with a screeching crumple of metal and bounced off to skitter along the road as I watched in my rearview mirror. Sarah gave a hic of terror when it hit, and put her hands over her ears.

I gunned the engine and picked up speed at once. Again I glanced in my mirror and saw Toombs still standing there, probably laughing his fool head off. "He's just trying to scare us," I said. Then, to myself, 'He's doing a damned good job.'

Sarah still had her hands over her ears. I reached over and pulled one of them down.

"Is he gone?" she said.

"He's gone."

"He'll never be gone."

"Unless he can run seventy miles an hour, he's gone," I said.

"He can do anything he wants," she said. The color was slowly coming back into her face.

"I'm going to get off the highway," I said. "He must have some way of tracking us when we take it."

"Where will you go?"

"I want to take S-1. That's this little road along the coast." I pointed it out on the map, keeping my eyes on the road ahead as I did so.

"This little curvy road here?"

I glanced over. "That's it," I said. "He won't be able to find us along that stretch, I'll bet."

"I wouldn't bet on a thing like that," she said seriously.

"Have you got a better idea?"

That shut her up.

From Genoa I hit it hard down through Varazze and the big seaport town of Savona, shifting often on the curves and swerving to avoid the annoying little vespas and mopeds and bicycles. This was not the road to make good time on, to be sure, but it was a switch from the highway, and I couldn't see how Toombs could anticipate our route, or intercept us along it. The countryside rose up abruptly from the ocean here, and left little room for maneuvering on his part.

The sun was falling farther over to the west now, striking a blinding glare into my eyes every time I looked in that direction. I realized how beautiful the view was along here with the long white beaches and the mountains and the blue water, and under different circumstances I would have commented it to Sarah. She was growing more and more strange, however, and I did not know quite what to say to her.

(Secretly I feared that having made love to her had somehow pushed her finally over the edge she had been clinging to so precariously).

We continued through Noli and Alassio and Imperia to the resort town of San Remo. "It won't be long now," I assured her.

"He could be anywhere," she said fearfully, glancing from side to side, "even in France."

Strangely, as she grew more and more afraid, I felt myself growing in courage. Are we not born for courage? Any beast of the field can plod along unawares and unsuspecting. It takes humankind to know, and yet to continue. We must face what lies ahead without cowering.

Perhaps I took my new boldness from her sudden lack of it.

Near Ventimiglia we crossed the Roia River, which was running high that year. On the other side we could see where a recent accident had taken place. There was glass slung along the road, and the guard rail next to the bridge had been uprooted. Apparently a car or truck had gone over the side. He must have been coming from the other direction, and slid down the embankment. I began to imagine what it must be like to die like that. It must have been terrible.

I mean, how long would it take before the crushed metal top of the car would smash the life from your body? How many times would you roll over and over inside the once friendly cab? Would you scream out your pain? Would you bite your tongue off?

I set these concerns out of my mind, finally, as we neared the French border, ten minutes later. Now we could be free.

When we were stopped I presented my papers and Sarah's passport to the uniformed guard. He gave her passport a cursory glance and handed it back. Then he became engrossed in reading the official papers that had been given me by the police in Verona. At last he looked up at me and shook his head. "I am sorry, monsieur, but it is impossible for you to pass into France with these papers."

"What do you mean? They were given to me in Italy. They're official papers. My passport was lost."

"You must get a real passport. You must return to Genoa.
There, you can get a new passport from the American Consulate."
"But you don't understand..." My heart was sinking.
"It is impossible for you to pass into France, monsieur."

NINETEEN

Had it not been for that one small detail - that of the missing passport, we might have slipped away into France and freedom. Instead, however, we found ourselves turning back toward Genoa. Our Fate was closing in upon us. There remained now only to see what that Fate might be. Perhaps we do deserve everything that happens to us, since it is only an extension of all our yesterdays.

"I'm beginning to believe he is a demon," I said. "Everything goes his way, doesn't it."

Sarah sat beside me with a stoney face. Her whole body was tensed and ready for what lay ahead. "Whatever happens," she said tersely, "remember that I love you. That's all that matters to me about any of this."

"I know you do," I said. "And I love you too."

"I'd go through it all over again, just to be with you. I'd endure anything to know a love like ours."

Her voice had taken on such a significant tone, I turned to look at her. "So would I," I assured her. "You're everything to me."

Now she looked at me and forced a little smile. "I think the only chance for happiness we have on this earth is through love. Do you think that's right?"

"I guess I hadn't thought of it, but yes, I do believe you've hit on something there."

We drove back through the same Ligurian countryside we had come through in the other direction only a short time before. After only a mile or so, we saw Morton Toombs standing alongside the road. He was on our side, holding his thumb out as if he might catch a ride. Surely he did not expect that we would stop for him...

As we approached the place where he stood I said to Sarah, "I ought to run him over."

"No," she said quickly. "You can't do that."

Even as I had said it, however, I knew that was exactly what I was going to do. I kept the car straight in the road as long as I could, (another force seemed to have taken over my hands), and

188

then, when he was only a few feet from my bumper, I swerved at him. Even then I might have swerved back to miss him if I had not seen that leering smile spread across his face. This was a man who needed to die. I remember bracing myself, waiting for the thud and then the body rolling up over the hood and into the windshield.

"Don't," Sarah screamed.

That was the last thing I remember for several moments. Apparently I missed Toombs completely, and hit a rock bank along the road. I don't know that for sure, (how could I have missed him?), but that is the only thing that makes any sense. If I had hit the man, he would have been crushed.

The sudden and unexpected impact had caused me to hit the windshield. When I came to after only a few seconds there was a webby spot in the glass before me. Looking into the rearview mirror, I saw a stream of blood running down my forehead and branching around the bridge of my nose. I was still quite disoriented. "Are you alright?" I asked Sarah, turning to look at her.

"I'm alright," she said. She, too, seemed dazed.

The sun was extremely bright now, and shining directly through her side window and into my eyes. My head throbbed. I reached out to touch Sarah's shoulder, when a shadow fell across the sun. I squinted to see what it was. It was Toombs.

Sarah reached over and quickly set the lock on her door. There was a moment's hesitation, and then the big man's fist came crashing through the window. A spray of broken safety glass showered over us. He took her by the throat. I heard her choking.

"Leave her alone you bastard," I yelled. I popped open the door on my side and stepped out of the car. Next thing I knew, I was laying on the side of the road. I had been so dizzy I simply fell over.

Toombs came around to my side, letting go Sarah's neck. "Get up," he said.

"I can't," I said weakly.

"Get up you scrawny punk." He jerked me up physically, with his one arm.

I sat there a moment, and then tried to scrabble away from him. He grabbed me again and picked me up off the ground altogether, and set me bodily into the seat of the car.

With surprising force he ripped open the back door, nearly taking the thing off its hinges, and got in.

"Drive," he ordered.

"I don't know if I can drive," I said, still feeling dizzy. I had begun to feel nauseous as well.

"Drive or I'll rip your fucking head off."

"Why don't you leave him out of it," Sarah said. "I'm the one you're after."

"You're both mine," he said. "It's too late for mercy now."

"It's never too late for mercy," Sarah told him. "Why don't you show a little. After all, it might keep you from having to go back."

Toombs laughed. It was a loud, roaring sound. "Why wouldn't I want to go back? I have it made."

"Someday you'll make a mistake and then you'll end up where you belong, burning in hell."

"I'll never make a mistake," he said. "If I can take the likes of you straight out of heaven, then by Satan's shaggy beard, I can take anyone."

"You might get a surprise one of these old days," Sarah said. I could hear by her voice, though, that she was resigned to what was going to happen. She was obviously powerless to do anything about it.

"I told you to drive," he said to me.

I started the motor and pulled out onto the road. All the while I was concentrating on keeping my head about me. The road seemed to rock back and forth drunkenly. I held the wheel tight and felt the sweat start to run all over my body.

"Where are we going?" Sarah asked.

"I think you know. I had you there once already. How you escaped, I'll never understand. Satan had you in his clutches. You can thank your gullible friend here for all that." With those words he reached up and cracked me across the back of my head with his left hand. I nearly fainted. I could not take much more of this.

"Leave him alone," Sarah snapped.

"What do you think you can do about it? Are you two lovers? Is that it. No wonder you don't have any power, my little angel. You can't have both, you know. You can either have mystic powers, or you can have love."

"You don't know anything," she told him. "You've never loved anyone or anything in your life. That's why you ended up in hell in the first place, remember."

"I do remember," he sneered. "I've always searched for power. That's why I steered clear of love. Love makes you weak. I want no part of it."

"Love can make you weak," Sarah agreed, "or it can make you strong. People in love can be twice as strong as a lonely old man. People in love can be more than twice as strong. It's a quantum thing, you see."

"I don't see any such thing," he snorted. "All I ever see is lovers tearing each other down."

"You've not looked hard enough then. There are still plenty of lovers willing to sacrifice everything for one another."

"Silly notions," he said.

While I concentrated on my driving, I could pick up only part of what was going on between the two of them. All of my efforts were going into keeping the car on the road. I was sorry I'd picked such a winding course now. I should have stuck with the Autostrada. I should have stayed on the straight and narrow. I never should have come here at all. I should have stayed home in Michigan where I belonged. Now look what I'd gotten myself into.

When I thought about what was going to happen next, my whole body began to shake. We were going to die. I didn't know how it would happen - whether with a gun or a knife or a shovel or with his bare hands, but I did know that the time was near. I was in such a disoriented state that I knew there was nothing I could do to prevent it. Sarah, though she was calm and controlled, seemed powerless too.

Five minutes passed. We were nearing the town of Ventimiglia.

"What's wrong with you, you snivelling coward!" Toombs pulled himself up on the back of my seat and shouted in my ears. Again he cuffed me and the pain caused black spots to form around the edges of my vision.

"I feel sick," I croaked.

"You don't feel nearly as sick as you will soon," he laughed again. His laughter was like a tidal roar in my head. I had never felt so weak in my life.

"I need rest," I insisted. I felt as if I would pass out at any moment.

"There will be no rest for you, son. Too bad you got caught up in all this, but it was your choice."

"My choice?" I said vaguely. "I don't remember any choice."

"You had the choice to go along as you were, in which case you would have remained safe. But you chose to involve yourself in things you did not understand. Now you're going to pay the price alright."

"The price?" I was losing my focus.

"We've reserved a special place for cowards. You've been a coward all your life. Didn't you think there'd be a price to pay for that. We'd have gotten you sooner or later, if you'd have stayed at home. This way we get you a little sooner, that's all." He laughed again.

"Don't listen to him," Sarah told me. "They can't hold you. If you wind up in hell, just cry out your faith in God and you'll be free from torment."

Toombs reached forward and punched Sarah in the face. He jerked my shoulder as he did so and I nearly ran the car off the road. We were in Ventimiglia now. Somehow I was able to settle the Ford back in the road. I glanced at Sarah. Her nose was bleeding but there was a look of open defiance in her eyes.

"What about you," I asked her. "Will you be able to get out."

"They have a special prison for me," she said. "I'll never get out."

We were approaching the Roia River bridge now. I could not think clearly. Our time was just about up. I knew I could not continue to drive much longer. My eyes were becoming more and more erratic; to such an extent that I almost could not keep the car in the road. The blow to the front of my head had caused me to lose track of my place in life.

Only one image came to me then. It was that of a rat caught in a rice paper maze. I could not, then, make anything of it. I could not remember where the thought had come from. I could not think of what it might mean.

As we neared the bridge, I knew that I could not cross back over it. We had come too far for going back. To recross the bridge now would mean permanent death. Somehow this idea came into my head.

Then I thought of the place that other car or truck had gone over the side. Perhaps they, too, had been unable to recross the bridge. Was this not, then, a significant dividing line?

The gap in the guard rail opened up by that other driver now became the central focus of all my attention. Since I could not recross the bridge, and since Toombs was only waiting for the appropriate moment to kill us both anyway, this hole in the railing seemed my only alternative. I aimed the car right for it.

"What are you doing?" Toombs said, again taking a shot at the back of my head with his hand. "Get back in the road there."

Out of the corner of my eye I saw Sarah turn to look at me. I glanced over. She was smiling.

"What the hell!" Toombs yelled.

I pressed on the accelerator with all my weight. The car lurched drunkenly forward, spurred on by the jolt of gas through the carburetor. We hit the gap in the railing precisely at its center. Toombs fell back into his seat, away from me.

For one long moment we were free. The car sailed out into thin air, as they say, throwing off the dynamics of gravity and earth and pavement. We were airborne. Weightless. Immune to any other concern. Free! Free! Free!

As in slow motion, I watched us nose downward. The river was below us. We hit the water. I was sucked forward against my will and again hit the glass of the windscreen. Belatedly I heard the crash of metal and glass. Water was pawing at my side window.

I reached over and tried to open my door. It would not budge. I looked over at Sarah. She was trying her door. It, too, was jammed tight.

Water began to rush in around the jimmied seals of the doors and in through Sarah's side window, (in a big way), and from some place under the dash. I could feel it pouring over my legs.

Toombs had been stunned for a moment by the crash, but he came awake now frantically. He clawed at each of the back doors in turn and then, finding them jammed, smashed out a window with his fist. The water rushed in all the quicker. There was no way to swim out through the window against the force of the current. "Sweet Satan!" he yelled once.

I turned to look at him. He began to scream in pain. Each place the water touched him peeled back like an extreme burn. His flesh bubbled up as if it was being boiled. His face became puffy and red. He continued to scream.

The car had tipped back a little in the river so that the water covered the back seat first. Toombs was up to his neck. His face seemed to melt away now, leaving only the startling white bone of his skull under it. He gasped his last breath and then was covered with water. There was a loud hiss, as when something hot is dipped in liquid, and steam was released. Toombs was no more.

My sense of triumph was short-lived, however. Water had now risen in the front up to our necks. I turned to Sarah. She was no longer attempting to escape. There was a look of total peace on her face.

The water was up to my chin. I tried to hold my face up, so as to catch every last breath of air. Once the car was completely under, I reasoned, and the water was no longer rushing in, we might be able to swim out the window. "We ought to be able to swim for it," I gasped, hoping Sarah would understand the rest of it for herself.

"It's no good," she said calmly. "We'll never make it."

"We've got to try..."

The water came up over my face now, and I nearly panicked. Then, sternly, I took control and forced myself to turn toward Sarah's broken side window and open my eyes. I pointed at it. She looked at me a long moment, then nodded, and swam for the window. She made it through.

I followed her out. Something snagged - my belt buckle perhaps. I reached down to free it. My air was running out. I couldn't hold my breath much longer. Again and again I tugged at the place but it was pinned fast.

My lungs were bursting for air. Sarah turned back and tried to swim to me. The current was too much for her. I was running out of air. I was dizzy from lack of air. I knew I could not last another moment.

Frantically I tugged and tugged at the offending belt, but it would not budge. 'Just my luck,' I remember thinking. 'Just my rotten luck.'

I began to let the air out of my lungs. I could not inhale, I knew. I simply could not inhale. Something was going to happen to get me loose from this window. Something was going to save me.

Sarah was being swept further away into the murk of the river. She could not get to me.

I couldn't last. It was over, I realized. I began to resign myself. I couldn't hold out another second. I inhaled.

There was the sound of flapping in my ears. Startled, I looked upward. Sarah was hovering above me with her great translucent wings moving forward and back as effortlessly as you please. She was smiling; and what a wonderful smile that was. Gracefully she picked me up in her arms and held me to her. I felt suddenly very safe. She rocked me back and forth gently. There was such tenderness in her motions that I leaned against her and put all my trust in her.

"I'll love you forever," she said.

"I'll love you more than forever," I said. "Take me to heaven with you."

"I can't," she said. "It's not time yet."

With those words I jerked awake. I was on the bank of the river and I could feel men's hands tugging me further ashore. I looked up. There she was, far off, all aglow and ascending toward heaven. I tried to wave but someone had hold of my arms. They were speaking rapidly in Italian. They were frantically trying to get out to the car.

Someone asked me a question, but I did not understand. Another man came over and asked in surprisingly good English, "Were there others in the car with you?"

"There were," I said, "but they're not there now."

"I'm sorry," he said, "I do not... a... understand."

I looked up into his face. His expression was so concerned I nearly laughed. After what I had been through, nothing of this earth seemed much to matter.

"It's alright," I said, "there's no one there."

TWENTY

An officer of the Carabiniere arrived and began to question me. I was still sitting on the bank of the river, shivering nervously. (I have never been good at answering the questions of officials). As I sat there I noticed a strange red-colored mist hanging in the shadows under the bridge. No one else, apparently, had seen it. No one asked anything about it, in any case.

"You were the driver of the car?" the officer asked me. He was poised with pen and paper - ready to record my responses.

"I don't remember anything," I said. "I hit my head."

The car was winched out of the water like an enormous dead frog. No drowned bodies were found. (Thank goodness - how would I have explained that?)

I remember thinking, 'I'm going to end up in the booby hatch if I tell them anything.' So of course I kept my thoughts to myself.

There were insurance papers to be filled out for the car rental agency. I was examined by a doctor. The whole place was in an uproar.

As you might imagine, I had developed a strange tendency to look up toward the sky. People were beginning to think me odd.

At last I was let alone, and I took a room in the Hotel Europa overlooking the sea. I began to hide out in there all the time. Several days passed as in a dream. People were going to start talking if they saw me looking up at the sky every other minute. Perhaps they would think me mad.

Indeed, I did feel myself right on the brink of a total breakdown. My mental state was extremely fragile. I needed time to think this through. Where, I needed to decide, did reality leave off and illusion begin? Or had I taken leave of my senses altogether. This, of course, was not a new idea for me.

Had I really met a woman named Sarah and had we been pursued by a psychopath named Toombs, or had all that been going on inside my head? And what of the events of these past days? Had I truly witnessed Toombs burn up in water and turn to vapor,

196

and had an angel really saved me from the wreckage of that car? Or, obversely, had I simply been swept ashore by the currents and dreamed the rest. You see what I mean; what sane person would not question such memories.

The late afternoon sun shone in my windows and turned everything dandelion yellow, but I scarcely noticed. I found myself sleeping a great deal, in order to keep reality out, I suppose. But the more I pondered what had happened, the less it seemed real to me.

Is it possible for the mind to analyze itself? one wonders.

Next morning I was going through the papers that had been in my wallet. I was putting them all back in their proper places. I had set them out here and there on the flat surfaces of the room to dry. Some had become so wet they were ruined, so I threw them away. There among them, however, my eye caught upon a white business card with raised black letters. At first I did not recognize it, and could not remember why I would keep such a card. Then I recalled - it was the card that had been given me by that old man I met back in London. The one who had called himself a teacher.

FREDERICH NAGEL, it read. PARAGON. Then it gave an address in Paris.

Yes, the man had said he was going to Paris, I remembered now. How long ago had that been? It seemed like ages, when in fact it had been less than two weeks. Was it possible that he was still in Paris?

I began to remember what Herr Nagel had said to me, those two weeks earlier. "If you are lost," he said, "I know the way." But of course he had been talking about the way to Victoria Station. Or had he?

"The world is full of strange and wondrous things," he had said. At the time I thought he was talking about tigers and elephants and such. Now, however, I was not so sure. I was a much more practical man back then.

"The trap is what you have just broken out of," he said when I became suspicious. "Now you can begin to understand yourself, and the world you live in."

Then, like a flash, I remembered the story about the rat and the rice paper maze. But for the rice paper walls standing between the rat and his freedom and understanding, he would not have been in a maze at all. He was being held in by his own perceptions.

I had wanted to learn, then, but had turned away from his teachings because I doubted. He did not seem to be the teacher I was looking for.

Next I thought, 'He was the first one to mention angels!' The minute I remembered that, I knew I had to find him. If I was going to discover answers for the questions that were running around in my head, I was going to have to get them from Herr Nagel.

Before I could depart for Paris, however, I had to return to Genoa to clear up the matter of my lost passport. I took the train up early the next day, saw the consular, got passport photos made, and was ready to leave again by the following morning. I then took the train over the mountain to Nice, a town surrounded by fields of flowers, and switched for Paris. Now that I'd made my mind up, everything else seemed to fall neatly into place. It seemed as if I was traveling along the path of my true destiny at last.

As the train bore me along toward that distant city, I began to think of Sarah. In the hustle and bustle of events following the accident, there had been no time to think of anything. Now, however, a sense of loss washed over me like a noxious wave. I did not know how I'd face the rest of my life without her.

I leaned back in the seat and closed my eyes, shutting out the everchanging scene that ran by outside the train windows. I had had enough of change. France continued, I am quite sure, but I took no part in her.

Sarah was gone now as if she had never been. In these last few hours she had been reduced to a phantom. I could not even remember the true color of her eyes. Our time together might have been illusion. Indeed, I had no proof that she had ever existed. I was as empty now as I had ever been. What kind of justice was that?

One never needs look far to find injustice, I suppose.

I arrived at the Gare de Lyon station in Paris in the late afternoon. Coming down the iron steps of the train and stepping out onto the station platform, I felt a thousand years old. My only luggage was the small overnight bag I had bought in Genoa, yet it seemed more than I could manage. Perhaps, I thought, I had made a mistake in coming here. What was I seeking, after all? What was done was done. All the tears the world could shed would not bring Sarah back. Certainly there was nothing this teacher could do.

Still, one must do something, and the pain is as unendurable in one place as another. I was being swept along toward the exit by the crowd. Besides, I reasoned, having made the decision to come here, and having actually come, I may as well see it through.

I took the Metro; line one to the Bastille, and then changed for line five, which took me to Gare d' Austerlitz, in the Fifth Arrondissement. The way seemed to have been paved for me. Actually, however, I have been in Paris before, during my time in the army, so I am not a complete stranger here. I had no trouble finding my way into the Latin Quarter.

The address, I discovered, was off the boulevard St- Germain on the Rue Bievre, so there was still some walking involved in finding it. Inwardly I was delighted to find myself in this part of the city with its many bookstores and cafes and literary types prowling the walks. I wondered if I would ever become part of it, as so many have before me. At last, turning toward the river, I found the house.

Frederich Nagel himself answered the door. There seemed to be no one else around. At first he did not recognize me. "Hello?" he said, looking closely at me with his piercing blue eyes. Apparently he deduced that I was American, since he greeted me in English.

"I'm the one..." I began lamely.

"Ah yes, the man with the angel," he said. Then, stepping aside, "Come in. Come right in."

I followed him in quietly. I didn't know quite what to say. He sat me down and poured me a cup of coffee. "I'm sorry that we got separated in Harwich," I said at last.

He waved away my little apology and launched right in. "Did your angel ever catch up with you?"

"It's true then?" I said hopefully. "You see, I was never sure she was an angel until right at the end. Even then..."

"So, you have some questions do you? Well, you've come to the right place. What happened with your angel? Tell me everything from start to finish."

As I told him the story he nodded and smiled or frowned, as was appropriate to my words, but said little. I finished up by saying, to my own revelation, "It was only when I crashed the car to kill Toombs, that she revealed herself to me. But then it was too late."

"Were you lovers?" he asked bluntly.

I nodded sadly.

"So you have embraced heaven in every way there is to embrace it," he said.

"Is that what I've done?" I replied. With every word of my story, I had felt my pain and sadness increase. "I miss her," I said, biting back my tears. "That's the only thing I know."

Herr Nagel was silent for some time. Then he said, "None of this has been adventitious, you know. Nothing happens by chance. There is a design to everything, whether you can see it or not."

"If it's not possible to see something, how do you know it exists?"

"I didn't say it was not possible to see it," he said patiently. "I only said that you could not see it."

"Is that what you teach?"

"It is the one true thing I know," he nodded. "But I am not really a teacher so much as a facilitator. When you are ready to learn a thing, I can point you in the right direction. The rest is up to you."

"I don't know what I'm ready for," I sighed.

Again the man paused a long moment, pondering what I had said. Then, "That may be the truest thing you have ever said."

"I've come for some answers," I said, feeling an unexpected sharp anger. "I haven't come for more puzzles and riddles. If you can't answer my questions, I might as well go."

"What is your question?" he asked calmly.

This stumped me. I opened my mouth to retort, but then closed it again. I had come all this way with some particular intent, I was quite sure, but now I couldn't remember what it was.

"Does it have to do with your angel?" he said.

"Yes," I blurted. My face turned red with embarrassment. "I want to know... I want to know if I will ever see her again."

"You will see her again," he said firmly.

"When?" I demanded.

"Soon," he said. "Think of it this way. Think about all time. How long has there been time?"

I thought about this for a moment, suspecting a trick, and then said, "Forever."

"And how long will time continue?"

"Forever," I repeated.

"And how long will you love this angel of yours?"

"Forever," I said yet again, without reservation. I began to reflect upon the word itself.

"So you see, the time we have here on earth is very brief. It is no more than a blink of an eye. In the blink of an eye, then, you will join your angel."

"I don't know if I can wait even that long."

"You must wait," he said. "There are other things you must do here on earth."

"What things?"

"That is what we must discover."

"Do you think it has to do with your Paragon?"

"It might," he said. "The fact that you have come all this way to find me suggests that it does."

"Alright," I said, resigning myself to what seemed to be my destiny, "but first you'll have to tell me something about it. Is it a religious cult?"

"No, not at all. Paragon is a way of thinking. It is a line of study. It is a game that parallels life itself. It is not intended to take the place of religious pursuits or other lines of study. No, not at all. It is meant to complement whatever else you may learn. It is meant to act as a unifying thread through your life."

"A thread isn't much to hang onto," I said.

He thought about this for a long moment. ("You see," he was to tell me later, "I am only a student myself.") After he had digested what I said, he replied, "Perhaps we had better call it a cord, then."

"Where does it come from, this Paragon? Is it something new. Did you make it up yourself?"

"It is very ancient," he said. His voice took on a reverent tone. "The ideas came from the heart of Asia, long before Buddha or Zen thought. Possibly it all originated in Shambala, the legendary city of the spirit. Who knows?

"The ideas spread throughout the world and are thought to be the precursor of all religious belief."

"Why is this the first I've heard of it then?"

"The various religions all went their own way, leaving the Paragon behind. But if you look closely, you will find many basic ideas that all religions have in common. That is what stems from the Paragon."

"Where did you learn of Paragon, then, if it was lost so long ago?"

"It was never completely lost. There has always been a dedicated group of students to keep it alive. The ideas have been handed down from one generation to the next in this way."

As he spoke, I noticed a strange thing happen. All of his years seemed to float away, and his face became that of a young man's. The world seemed to lose its hold, and I could see his true spirit, still youthful and vital, showing through.

He explained to me, then, how our modern life had become a rather two-dimensional affair, devoid of that important spiritual plane that lies just beyond our grasp. "In other times," he said, "humankind walked with the spirit in daily life. Now, however, we are divorced from that world. Anything that does not fall within the realm of the physical, the intellectual, the scientific, or the strictly logical, is forgotten. We simply have no time for it."

This, he explained, has left a wide rift in our lives that we attempt to fill with pat little sayings, parables, magic, cults, and pop religions. "Modern people are looking for a 'quick fix', to use a word that is, I think, from American terminology. They don't want to put the time and effort into finding the true way. Everyone wants everything right now, and it just doesn't work that way."

"Knowledge without wisdom," I interjected.

"Exactly right," he nodded. "Paragon encourages the search for knowledge, and thus wisdom."

"Some people are afraid of knowledge," I said.

"Yes, they are. And that is sad. They ignore all that is going on around them. But every person experiences the world differently; no two are alike. All things and all people have something to teach you, if only you are willing to listen. Why should you dwell upon only what you know, when there are so many others who know something else. People should be curious about what others think. It would give them a whole new perspective on life."

"You mentioned something about a game," I said. "I don't see how a game could fit into all this. What is that about?"

"Ah, the game. You see, Paragon is not all serious, any more than life itself can be. There is wonder, and mystery, and even comedy. Playing the game, to put it simply, is a correlative of human experience. Much has been made of it by some, however, and one could spend too great a part of his time on the game, and forget about the ultimately more important stuff of life."

"What sort of game is it?" I asked.

"It is an interactive game - not just between two players, but between the players and the world of the spirit. One author came very close to describing the process correctly. That was Hermann Hesse. If you have not done so, you must read his 'Glass Bead Game'. Then you will begin to understand."

"Was Hesse a member of Paragon?"

An evasive smile crossed the man's face. "Not, perhaps, in the way you mean. We do not pledge allegiance to some central authority or rule. We all come to Paragon in our own way. We all have our own talents. Hesse knew of Paragon, and he advanced its ideas. So in a way, yes, he was a member."

"Who else?" I asked expectantly. I began to think of others who might have been part of this exclusive club. Perhaps, I was thinking, I would become connected with the great minds of history through association.

"There are many others," he replied cryptically, "but we had better wait for another time to reveal them. I am sure that you could name many of them, if you consider their accomplishments."

"I'll bet I've read some of them," I said. "I'm a writer too, you know."

"They're not all writers by any means," he said. "But yes, I'm sure you have. Their ideas are integral parts of the advancement of civilization. In that same way, perhaps yours will be too. Who knows?"

"I've always hoped I could be part of something like that. I never thought it would happen, though."

"We are all in the constant process of becoming," he said. "You must remember, however, that all of the various lines of our inquiries intersect at Paragon. That is the true meaning of what we do. We do not become caught up in our own little world of study. There is always a place where it meets the Paragon."

"I'll remember," I vowed.

"You will be a good gamesman, I'm quite sure. You have proven already that you are able to hold onto your sanity while reaching for the unknown. Not everyone can do that. The game allows you to approach life from without, you see. You must be versatile to play it."

"There were times I thought I was going out of my mind," I admitted.

"Of course, of course. We have all been to that edge. The key is to know where it lies, and not go beyond."

"I wonder," I said, "do you think it would be possible for me to write about Paragon itself. Has that ever happened? I've never read anything about it."

"If you feel that is what you must do, then, yes, by all means, write."

"It's probably only fair to tell you," I continued, "I've never been published before."

Herr Nagel laughed. "In this day and age, that is almost a recommendation in itself. So much of what is published now is trash, as you well know. Entertaining trash, some of it, but still trash. And how the critics rave over it..."

"Still, one always feels accepted when he has published."

"We'll see to it that you are published," he said. "The fact is, we've been hoping for a writer for some time. It's about time our ideas are brought to light."

"I'm surprised they've not been published before."

"The ideas themselves have always found a voice, but the Paragon has remained hidden. We think now, however, that the world is going to self-destruct if we don't come forward. Perhaps it will anyway, who knows? I only hope it is not too late. The earth is becoming an empty cell, isolated from the greater Universe around it."

"Still," I reflected aloud, "I wouldn't know where to begin such a story. If it's as ancient as you say, the number of tales must be nearly infinite."

"You could start with the story you already know, your own."

"What? My story is not so important as that of the Paragon, I'm quite sure."

"Behind the obvious plot of your own story, the true plots are lurking. You have already lived it. Now you must write it down."

Again I began to object. "Surely there are other..."

"Yours," he interrupted, "is one of the greatest stories I've ever heard. The coming together of a man and his angel... it's incredible really. I hope you don't mind my saying, it is one of the great stories of all time."

"I don't mind," I said, "but, to tell the truth, I'm not sure yet if I believe the story myself. How am I going to get others to believe me?"

"That is a dilemma," he said, "but I'm sure you'll figure a way. You're a practical man, aren't you?"

"I always thought I was, until a few weeks ago. Now I don't know what I am."

"You're a man who has begun to learn. Don't pull back now."

"Still," I insisted, "I hadn't really thought I'd be writing about myself, or my own experiences. I'm a private sort of person. I'll have to give it some thought."

"Certainly," he said, "you'll need some time to decide where you stand on all this. But please, when you have decided, write that book. It's bound to be a great one."

Without further delay, then, I excused myself and went out for a walk. As I walked along, I began to ponder all of the things that had happened in my life since I decided to leave my secure position in the construction trades. Looking back, I realized how I had been building my self one floor at a time, without the possibility of deviation. Everything I did followed a kind of predetermined blueprint. Had I stayed, I would have walled myself in completely and irrevocably.

So I had broken out of my old pattern, somehow, and had come to Europe and met my own angel. How incredible that sounds, even now!

How could I be sure it had ever happened? What if it all turned out to be some elaborate hoax. What if the whole thing was unreal, and that I too was an unreal part of it. The more I thought along this line, the more my mind wheeled down into a kind of mental whirlpool.

What if the story had made me up? Then I would be but a character of someone else's creation. What if the reader was not reading at all, but was somehow projecting these words onto the tabula rosa - the blank page, without even knowing it.

You can see, I think, how my mind was reeling out of control.

If there was only some way now of reassuring myself that it had all been true. That it had not been but a silly figment of my imagination. (You see how even proof in the flesh was not enough). But where could such reassurance come from? I wondered.

I was walking along with my head down, concentrating only on my own thoughts. A dull ache was developing in the front of my head, just above my eyes. What a quandary I was in. I could see no way out of it.

Without thinking to look, I stepped out into the next intersection. There was a sudden and startling squall of tires braking across the pavement. I turned to see a blue Citroen bearing down from the left. It slued somewhat sideways as it came. I could see the look of fear on the driver's face, though strangely I felt no fear myself. There was not time to be afraid, I suppose.

This was one of those moments when time seems to come to a standstill. I lurched back, hoping against hope that I could somehow escape this unkind fate, but anyone could plainly see that the car was going to hit me. Then, as if defying the very laws of nature, my body flew back and I landed on my back on the sidewalk. I was unharmed, I realized with surprise.

At that moment I heard the sound of wings in my ears, and my heart soared.

AUTHOR'S NOTES

More than two years have passed since I began to write this record of my journey toward liberation. It has been a time of profound loneliness but also one of learning and development. By adding these few pages, however, I do not mean to continue my story or to further clarify any particular point in what I have already said. Instead, I would like to introduce the manuscript I am currently working on.

The task of linking my works together is an intricate one, I am finding. A puzzle piece that might connect one to the next must be large and oddly-shaped. It is often a long step between them, to put it plainly. That is because of the many facets to be found in Paragon, and the multitude of people who are now, or have once been, involved in it. As I have stated in the text, the ideas of Paragon are very ancient.

"The ideas spread throughout the world and are thought to be the precursor of all religious belief," Herr Nagel had said.

How, then, can I hope to bind all of the diverse parts of this subject together in a single master work? You can see my dilemma, I am quite sure. One literary devise I could employ is to simply string all of the various works together in a series; each beginning where the last left off. To be comprehensible the reader would be forced to read them in the order they are written. The trouble with that particular method, however, is that the shear number of volumes might eventually become unwieldy. A new reader would be forced to buy and read eight or ten volumes, let us say, before he or she could pick up the latest one. That would make the important ideas of Paragon inaccessible to all but the most devoted reader. This, of course, is not my intention.

For this very reason I have chosen to group these various records together in a literary cycle. That is, each will be related to the central subject; the Paragon, while they may not be directly related to one another. Some historic figures and even modern-day members will show up time and again, and of course my own voice will act as a common thread for all, but each volume will be expected to stand on its own, and thus can be read separately. A

reader is free to pick up at any point along the chain and explore
forward and back, or even skip around at will. That, in essence,
is the very nature of learning, is it not? Seldom do we proceed
along well-defined paths to understanding.

But enough on that subject! We must proceed. The
manuscript I am now working on is the story of a man we have
already met. He is Daniel Allman, the owner of a London
curiosity shop. He is a relative newcomer to Paragon, but one who
has learned its lessons incredibly fast. His learning, in fact, has
far outstripped his power and ability. When his daughter is
kidnapped by a powerful sorcerer, then, his strength of faith is to
be severely tested. In order to play this particular game, he is
forced to visit a distant region. It is a region where mind and
matter converge. It is a place of Mirabilia.

Here's how it begins:

Even as he opened his eyes Daniel knew that the
extraordinary had at last occurred. As far as he knew only
his teacher, (the one who led the charmed existence), had,
in recent history, traveled in this incredible manner. Certainly
he himself had never before accomplished this singular leap
in understanding. But then, never before had he found himself in such dire circumstance.

He was on a night-shrouded beach. The ocean was
behind him; the jungle before him. There was only enough
of a moon for him to see the horizontal whites of the waves
on the sea, and the tops of the shaggy palms pressed against
the sky ahead. The darkness of the treeline was flashing
with the pin-point multitudes of soundless bouncing fireflies.

Having landed unglamorously on his hands and knees
in the sand, the man now stood up. Yes, it was true, the
unexplainable had happened. His capacity for wonder, which
had for so long been dulled by the banality of his life,
suddenly bloomed within him in a rain-drenched cactus flower
fascination. He looked about himself with a renewed sense
of awe.

Having thrust himself headlong into this world of
dreams, he had the feeling that he had only just awakened
from his dream, and that what he now saw was, in fact,
reality. He knew intuitively that he could never recover what
he had been, and could only go forward from here, no matter

how strange his future might become. His experiences from now on could either debilitate or enlighten him, depending entirely upon himself and his own actions.

***

But I mustn't offer more than a taste. What happens from there is an astonishing tale of danger and courage and, ultimately, the clash between the powers of good and evil. How Daniel Allman conducts himself in this mythic thriller will determine whether he survives or perishes. I call it MIRABILIA, which is the Latin word for miracles.

Since my association with Paragon, I have learned many wondrous things, and I am sure I will learn many more. Every moment of life, it seems, is filled with the surprise and adventure and beauty of the very first moment. I have learned that we have access to spiritual forces that are beyond our wildest imaginings. I have learned that we must open ourselves to this other dimension if we are not going to extinguish completely the great mysteries of existence. With these things I have also learned many amazing and moving stories. There are so many, in fact, that I only hope I live long enough to tell them all.